To Rick and Connie,
Hope you like my
story -
Fred D. Fortune
12-31-2023

D1738153

TABLE OF CONTENTS

PREFACE

Barriers raised by customs and traditions confront all, but for some it is insurmountable. Henry David Thoreau said it succinctly when speaking of how deep and rugged the marks are of custom and tradition. Many have felt trapped by these ancient ways, but there are others who escape the very circumstances in which they are cast.

John Oxenham declared there are three ways for every man. The high soul takes the high road the low soul takes the low road and the rest drift too and fro on the misty flats. But every man "Decideth" the way he should go. There are many others who follow the thought, "Let's just go with the flow of the current and see where it takes us." Truthfully, there are currents and challenges in every life, but the greatest peril we face is to do nothing with what we have been given. Intelligent people have oft been heard to say, "It's not the gales but the set of the sails that determines the way the ship goes." But at the crossroads of every life there is a common denominator, it is choice.

It has been said there are three main choices in life. The first and foremost has to do with a belief in the Creator, the second is who your life's mate will be and the third and final is what you will do with your life's occupation. They are all critical to your success and happiness as a human being. Make no mistake about it, the choices above have consequences, and one is eternal.

Billy McGovern, my fictional character, is gifted and intelligent.

His destiny requires a choice. Billy's destiny of choice takes him through both dangers and happiness. But he makes the choice.

I do not remember why I ever started to compose this book and especially at my age, since I am now an aging senior. But it has been a pleasure to live with Billy, Betty Jane, Glen and all my other fictional characters. They have at times brought emotion to my eyes.

I offer a word of thanks to a sister, who read my story and offered encouragement and suggestions, and to my editor,

Jeffrey Dierkes, for his work. I would also mention Trisha Dreher, my artist and G Glen Farrier, who has been a source of encouragement in several respects. I hope you will enjoy my story. I have enjoyed my work.

PART I

A DESTINY OF CHOICE

1828 was a restless year for many in Europe. Young folks, especially the poor class, were looking for new beginnings. What they found was a stagnant society controlled by dynasties of older generations with wealth. The poor class with a vision, dreams and imagination found little opportunity for fulfillment. For them it was a society of two classes, the rich and the poor. Because of these conditions, many let circumstances and situations control their destiny, never thinking they might do something about it.

The McGovern's imagination of a better way of life brought them to the North American continent. Like so many immigrant families coming to the shores of America, they were optimistic of finding land they could call their own. A place where they and their family could grow with the land. It was a dream they did not yet possess; it was a dream of what might be. It would be for their children, and it would be costly. The McGovern's made the choice

The family had crossed the Atlantic reaching their Philadelphia destination and had temporarily settled in the state of Pennsylvania. It was in Pennsylvania they met a fine Dutch family named Swearengen. There was an immediate bond between the two families, most particularly between the women folk. They were strangers in a new land, the companionship of the two families was priceless for the ladies. The Scottish brogue and the Dutch dialect were difficult obstacles initially, but the two women managed it in time. They shared in every way they could.

Since neither family found Pennsylvania to their liking, they began to look elsewhere. The influx of new people coming to America, plus people already desiring more land, brought about an ever-expanding population to the West. This created opportunity for some and terrible hardships for others. Tennessee was a classic example.

The year 1830 had been a year of two important Acts of Congress affecting the state of Tennessee. First, and most important for the two families, the Land Grant Act passed in January. It allowed the purchase of land tracts for 12 1/2 cents per acre. To whom did this land belong? Quite simply it belonged to Native Americans. The Native Americans were considered savages, and they could and would be removed. Andrew Jackson saw to it.

Secondly, in March, the Indian Removal Act was passed. The Act stipulated Native Americans were to move west of the Mississippi on land provided. The tribes most affected were the Cherokee, Creek, Choctaw, Chickasaw and the Seminole. This Act created painful hardships and heart-rending difficulties for the natives. It triggered one of the ugliest events ever implemented by our ancestors, The Trail of Tears.

The Indian Removal Act proved to be massively devastating for the Indians. Between 1831 and 1877 an estimate 60,00 to 100,000 Native Americans were moved west of the Mississippi to make room for white settlers. It was a bitter pill for the Native Americans.

Davy Crockett, then a Congressman from Tennessee, opposed the Act. There were differing reasons suggested for Crockett's disapproval; ranging from Crockett's distaste of Andrew Jackson, his sympathy for the Cherokee and some even venture to say it was political.

It was said here was compensation paid the Natives. But it is a fact that little ever reached the Natives. There was another way the price would be paid. There were continuing raids on wagon trains traveling west. But by the mid-1860s most Indian raids had ceased on Oregon wagon trains.

There were however still some occasional raids from renegade bands. These bands were made up of Native Indians who had an intense hatred for what had been done to their people in the Indian Removal Act. Their nomadic way of survival, often including raiding anyway, made it easy for them to plunder the hated wagon trains. There were some wagon trains that simply were never heard of again.

The McGovern's had heard of property in Northwest Tennessee for a reasonable price and had shared their interest with the Swearengens. Very soon afterward the two families left for Northwest Tennessee. By the fall of 1831 they settled near Dyersburg, both McGovern and Swearengen families acquired adjacent land tracks of 640 acres. The two families shared in the backbreaking task of establishing their homesteads. There were also Indian attacks in which the two families fought side by side.

When 1860 came, the second-generation men had both heard of the new repeating rifle, the Henry. The Henry was unique in that it was the first breech loading lever action rifle. It carried a load of fifteen cartridges and one in the chamber. By 1863 both Jacob

McGovern and Joshua Swearengen had made a major decision. While their decision was made for protection against the natives, their purchases would have far-reaching effects for both families and especially for the McGoverns.

Both men had purchased the new Henry. The Civil War found both men in the battle of Chickamauga, on September 18, 1863. It was a battle that would be second only to Gettysburg in loss of life. The Confederates would win the three-day battle, but not before Jacob McGovern had taken a Union bullet directly in the chest on the first day of battle. Lying in a small area of cover, Jacob knew his end was at hand.

Joshua Swearengen knelt close by Jacob. With his last breath Jacob begged Joshua, "Josh if you make it back would you care for my family, tell Mary I love her, and look after my son Billy and I want him to have the Henry." Those were the last words Jacob would ever speak, he was gone.

Joshua would keep his word, giving Billy the Henry, and go a step further. Something of significance import happened at the close of the war. Joshua, though wounded, had survived the war. On the day of his return, he happened across a sizable cache of abandoned .44 caliber cartridges.

Someone else had tasted death never to return to his store of ammunition. Out of deep respect for Jacob and family, the ammunition would benefit both families. Joshua decided to split the .44's with Billy. Joshua's act of kindness is understandable, but what he did not know was the place the gift would play in the McGovern future.

At first light the morning after his return from the war, Joshua and Hilda Swearengen made their way to the McGovern farm. They had anticipated with dread the impact the terrible news would bring to Mary and young Billy. Mary McGovern had seen their approach, sensing something terrible had happened she was stricken with panic. Billy but 14 years old, sensing the moment had taken his mother in his arms.

When the Swearengens entered the home, there were no words spoken. Mary and Hilda burst into tears. Later Joshua would share the last minutes of Jacob's life with Jacob's family. Billy, not realizing it, took the place of a man and addressed the Swearengens, "Mr. and Mrs. Swearengen, my mother and I are deeply grateful for your kindness." Later when the Swearengen's were parting,

Billy spoke alone to Joshua, "Thank you for returning Dad's gun and the ammunition you have sacrificed, I have a feeling it will mean much to us in the future." On the way home Joshua commented to his wife, "Hilda, Jacob's boy Billy speaks beyond his years." Hilda nodded her head in solemn agreement.

Billy who had been large for his age, had worked the farm since his father joined the Confederate Army. It had been terribly difficult at first and it had been done without complaint. Billy would continue to do so, but Mary had been unable to recover from the loss of Jacob.

Mary gradually declined in health and after struggling four brutal years she passed on November 10, 1867. Billy's neighbors, the Swearengens, swore she died of a broken heart. Mary, aware Billy would be alone, made a last request of Billy. "Billy, my brother William Richards lives in Sacramento I wish you to go to him. William will look after you."

Joshua and Hilda Swearengen could not understand Mary McGovern's plea made to young Billy. Joshua commented too Hilda, "He's only a lad, how will he ever reach California? Look what he will be sacrificing." Hilda continued the line of thought, "Do you realize it will be the first break between our two families in three generations.?" Joshua continued the conversation, "When Jacob was in his last moments, he asked that I look after Billy. Hilda, I am sitting down with Billy to have a man-to-man conversation. I don't believe Jacob would approve of this move."

A few days later Joshua did just that, "Billy, I don't believe your father would approve this move you're making, have you thought of that?" Billy gave the following answer, 'I have thought it over carefully, I will be honoring my mother's wish. My future is in California, and I am determined to see what's leading me west to Sacramento." Billy had made his choice to move to California. The fact was Billy was completely alone at the age of eighteen, and the choice was his to make.

It was true the Swearengens had heard of the difficulties faced between Dyersburg, Independence and Sacramento. It was over 2,400 miles of unsettled land. The trip would take six to seven months over the harshest land ever seen, many never made it. Mary McGovern never knew what she was asking of Billy, of this the Swearengen's were quite sure.

After inheriting the very dream of his ancestors and owning a successful farm, Billy was sacrificing it all. He would be starting over. The Swearengen's knowing what Billy was giving up and what he would be facing, tried in vain to convince him differently. Billy was steadfast in keeping his promise to his mother and following what he believed to be the right move.

After thinking it over carefully Billy sold land and stock to the Swearengens. Billy knew they would stand good on the payment. The sale of the property and livestock was prompted when Billy had gotten word of a wagon train departing from independence, Missouri for Sacramento, California.

Billy did not like the prospect of carrying the full amount of cash on the trip West and the Swearengen's did not have the full amount anyway. He made an agreement with them. The telegraph business was new and expanding. It would serve the purpose later. Billy knew the Swearengen's would not let him down.

Billy was unable to part with Arkie, a beautiful sorrel quarter horse bought from a family who had plans of heading west. The horse had been a mere colt and the family did not want the task of an extra horse not useful to them in travel. Jacob bought the horse for Billy just before leaving for war.

The horse and Billy were inseparable. Arkie was now four years old, stood 14-and-one-half hands, had a wide head, a muscular chest and was extremely fast. Arkie was attentive to every command by Billy, he knew Billy's whistle at a distance. The horse was gentle by nature and friendly to humans. He was a splendid animal with a slight bit of thoroughbred in him and he could run. Billy spoke right out to Arkie, "Arkie we're headed West." Arkie looked at Billy and nickered.

Billy McGovern carried the responsibility of the McGovern dream. Billy had in solitude dealt and concluded the McGovern dream was not fulfilled with the successful farm near Dyersburg, Tennessee. Moving on was not the choice of his mother, but his choice. Billy was very much aware of what he was doing. He had dealt with three age old concepts in making his decision. The past, the present and the future. For the past it was not what Billy alone had done, but what his father had done and the McGovern's before them had done.

The present was fine, but neither were for Billy, they were not the dream. The dream was in the future.

Billy knew it would be over twenty-four hundred miles to Sacramento and he knew he would face difficulties; he even knew some of the difficulties he was sure to face. But with all that said, Billy innately knew it was the thing he would do, it was the thing he should do. It was 440 some odd miles from the farm in Dyersburg, Tennessee to Independence, Missouri and he had better get a move on.

Billy reckoned if he and Arkie could make twenty miles a day, it would take twenty-two days to reach Independence. He would leave as soon as he could. If any luck he would catch the California wagon train, he would depart first light tomorrow. Billy, Arkie, and all Billy's earthly possessions left for Independence, Missouri on a bright Monday morning, March 30, 1868.

Billy and Arkie crossed the Mississippi at Caruthersville on a small ferry. Billy was concerned how Arkie would react to travel on the ferry, Arkie just nickered and nosed Billy's shoulder. Arkie seemed to know if he was with Billy, he was ok. After crossing the Mississippi Billy took a route north to miss the Ozark Mountains then headed due west to Independence. There was ample water along the way and travel progressed as Billy had hoped.

It was the later part of April by the time Billy reached Independence, the California wagon train had left the week before. Because of the late date there would not be any more California wagon trains until next year. There was, however, a late train leaving in two days for Oregon. Billy reckoned the California train would travel the Oregon trail to Fort Hall in the Idaho Territory then turn south through Nevada following the Humboldt River for a good part of the way and then over the Southern Sierra Mountain range on to Sacramento,

California. If the Oregon train made reasonable time, he would catch the California group after departing from the Oregon train in Idaho. It was Billy's plan.

Billy had met Ben Thompson, Wagon Master of the Oregon group, and was well pleased. Ben, knowing young Billy was alone, had invited Billy to have an evening meal with him and some associates on the eve of their departure for Oregon. Ben's associates were experienced Wagon Masters. Their knowledge would prove vital for Billy.

One of Ben's associates Billy met, Glen Forester, would travel with them on the

Oregon wagon train. Both Ben and Glen were men of experience and took an immediate liking to Billy. Glen especially like the youngster, remarking to Ben later, "Something special about him." Glen was a straightforward type of man, not obnoxiously inclined, but one who could be counted on for the truth.

The meeting itself was filled with conversation, laughter, stories, and bits of knowledge of wagon travel that unfortunately would never be heard again or ever put to a pen. Billy was perceptive and instinctively knew the men he was listening to with respect and appreciation. They were men of stature. Their words would be worth keeping.

One important comment escaping Billy's thinking completely was made by Glen. Much later Billy would recall Glen's remark. Glen reported, "One thing about that departed California wagon train, never saw a young lady that beautiful before." Three other men had remarked the same sentiment, she was indeed a beautiful young lady.

Billy listened carefully to several of these men. One was very perceptive sizing Billy up. He turned to Billy and said, "Young man you're a listening awful careful." Billy was embarrassed and momentarily froze. Glen stepped to Billy's rescue, "He's with Ben and me, he will be going on to California alone." Glen continued telling in a few words Billy's past. When he finished, the men looked upon Billy with admiration. Ben had noticed how quickly they took him under wing. Especially when they understood after leaving the Oregon train, he would venture on to California alone.

Andrew Winstead, the wagon master who had embarrassed Billy, was embarrassed himself after realizing the impact of his words. Knowing Billy would cover Nevada and Donner's Pass, he shared valuable insight with Billy. Billy said, "What you have told me is important. I wish to thank you for every word you have spoken." Andrew stood tall before Billy and said, "Young man, I want you to have this." When finished speaking he stood before Billy, his eyes softening, and he unfastened his Colt revolver and holster, and handed it to Billy. It was a beautiful gun, and it was a treasured gift. You could tell by looking it had received exceptional care. Billy knew what the man was offering but was reluctant to take something he had never earned. Glen stepped next to Billy, "Take it, he wants you to have it. He knows you will need it." Billy believed Glen, and somehow, he knew he was receiving one of the most important gifts he would ever receive. Andrew Winstead saw in Billy's eyes a deep appreciation for the gift. Andrew Winstead felt something he had not experienced in a long time. He knew by the look in young Billy's eyes he would never be forgotten. For him, his active sharing was heartwarming. While he did not know the words, Billy knew he was in the presence of a caring, compassionate man, who was looking into Billy's future. The man read Billy thoughts. Billy could tell by the looks of the revolver it had received careful attention; he knew he would do the same. The old gentleman was sure of it.

Billy met a friendly, congenial couple, William, and Milly Dreher. William and Milly were likewise traveling with the wagon train. When the Dreher's discovered Billy was traveling alone, Milly spoke out quickly. "Billy McGovern, would you like to travel with us?" Without hesitation, Billy answered, "Mr. and Mrs. Dreher, that is truly kind of you. And if you will let me provide the meat for your wagon, I will be happy to travel with you.

The prospect made both parties happy. This worked out well for Billy, he liked the Dreher's from the get-go, they were a kind, home spun couple considerate of others. Jacob McGovern had once told him, "Son, you find people who care for others, you found some good human beings." Billy had cherished his father's advice. In fact, there would always be a special place in Billy's memory of the words his father spoke.

The Dreher's liked Billy and since their home had never been blessed with the youngsters, Mrs. Dreher was very partial to Billy. Billy I could tell by the large piece of pie, and the kind expression in Milly Dreher's eyes, she favored him. In all, it was comforting, and a pleasant relationship Billy was not apt to forget.

It was 1868, they were four days out of Independence, when wagon master Ben Thompson discovered Billy's accurate Henry. Ben was not a novice. It was his third trip west, and his experience warned him to size up his men folk as soon as possible.

Ben was extremely grateful for Glen's accompanying the train at the last moment. Ben had important positions left vacant by two cancellations the day before his departure. Ben's well-chosen horseman would be unable to travel because of a heart problem. This was filled by old friend Glen Forester, an able-bodied person whose knowledge Ben knew of firsthand from previous travel. Glen could do the rigors of daily travel on the trail; broken wagon wheels, thrown horseshoes, and other difficulties. Glen knew how to take care of them without any problem. The other vacant positions worried Ben. He found no one to replace his scout. Ben would have to make do.

Ben had not missed Billy's every day return with fresh game for the Dreher wagon. Ben, who had never been backward about being forward, did not waste any time enlisting Billy. "Billy, I'm in need of someone to provide meat for the wagon folk." Billy looked carefully at Ben and answered, "Give me a little time to think about it." Ben Thompson knew what Billy was doing. Billy was taking careful stock of how much ammunition he had on hand. Billy might have declined the offer, but for the additional .44 cartridges Joshua Swearengen had given him. Once more the thought flashed through Billy's mind, how helpful the Swearengen's had been. Consequently, Billy had the Henry and enough ammunition to last for some time. He would take the responsibility Ben laid at his doorstep. On the very next occasion, with very alert eyes, Billy responded "Mr. Thompson, I will do what you ask of me." Ben quickly added, "Would you also keep a sharp eye out? I need a scout." Billy answered. "I will do my best."

Not everyone was happy with Ben's choice. Jake Heilman was 21 years of age. Knowing Ben would need helpful men, Jake was anxious of a place of import. Jake liked being looked up to and was not reluctant to push his cause. Ben's choice of Billy had stuck in Jake's craw. Billy had seen Jake's attitude by the ugly looks of jealousy cast his way. It had not bothered Billy.

Before many days passed, Billy had made acquaintance with four other young men with the train, all ranging from 16 to 19 years old. Billy McGovern, James Offlander, Isaiah Swartz, Melvin Petersen, and Jeremy Welmont all had something in common. Each owned or had access to a Henry rifle.

Later Isaiah asked Jimmy, "Is Billy as good with that Henry as I've heard?" Jimmy responded, "Isaiah, I've never seen anyone better. We can learn from him.   Billy was incredibly good with the Henry. With Ben's approval, the boys took turns assisting Billy on the daily routine hunts. After a month on the trail,

Billy had taught the other young men how to lead the game before firing, to gauge wind velocity and distance. After which they became quite adequate and competent marksmen. Jake Heilman was not happy with this.

Billy had some sort of a premonition this might come in handy in the future. For this reason, Billy shared with the four other young man a conversation he had carefully listened to among Ben and several other Wagon Masters on the eve of their departure from Independence. Specially from Andrew Winstead who gave Billy the .45 Colt revolver. Several things he said remained in Billy's thinking.

Jimmy, Isaiah, Melvin, and Jeremy had learned a deep respect for anything they received from Billy. The lessons and their marked improvement with the Henry rifle made them believers in Billy. They listened intently when Billy related what Andrew Winstead had said, "Indians of stature liked additional feathers of color, they rode better horses usually larger. When the Indians found a weak spot in the wagon train, they gave a shrill signal indicating to the other braves their line of attack. Usually, they stayed out of range until the frightened wagon train folk were reloading their rifles. The Indians attack would then be swift, brutal, and annihilating every living thing."

Billy had shared this with each of the young men on their separate hunts. "If ever under attack, you would do well to pick out these Braves first. It could be the deciding factor in the raid."

Billy, and no one else in the wagon train, knew they were being watched. However, on the early dawn of the Indian attack, Billy and Jimmy Offlander were hunting game when two things happened. First, Arkie stopped short, snorted, pawed the earth, and nodded toward the East. Billy knew immediately Arkie sensed something threatening. Next, Jimmy pointed out unshod Mustang tracks at a considerable distance. There was a piece of sod sticking up, few would have noticed. Jimmy said, "Billy, let's go take a look at those tracks." After looking, they knew they had to pursue the tracks further. The boys took a careful chance and found the war party moving in the direction of the wagon train. Billy and Jimmy had not been discovered. They immediately returned to the wagon train before it broke camp. "Ben, there are thirty Choctaw Warriors hard on our track, ready to attack." Ben Thompson wisely and quickly decided it would be best to delay their early start and keeping the wagon train in a tight circle. Ben Thompson spoke out to the entire wagon train in a thunderous voice, "We are about to be attacked by a band of Choctaw warriors. I want women and children inside the wagons on the floor immediately. Men with muzzle loaders under the wagons. Let's move."

Three Bears and twenty-nine other warriors had moved into position, and after tracking and familiarizing their party with the wagon train patterns, he planned their attack for dawn. It would be the third massacre led by Three Bears. He had gained quite a reputation among a small tribe of Choctaw people who were remnants of what had so brutally gone before.

Three Bears knew the wagon train would be well stocked with fine horses, food, rifles, ammunition and all the items needed by his people. Three Bears had been careful to track at a farther distance than ever before not wanting to be discovered. He had been correct.

They had been aware of the young men who each day hunted and their skill in hunting. The singular shots of the young men had not bothered Three Bears.

Three Bears believed in his ultimate success, he estimated twenty to twenty-five men on the wagons, and he had every confidence in his ability to annihilate the wagon train. Fifteen of his twenty-nine Braves were excellent in every respect. They knew exactly what to do and when to do it. By the third round of the wagons the additional rifles would be empty, and reloading would be slowed considerably. The Indians who had stayed just on the edge of the accuracy range would then move closer taking deadly advantage of their accurate bowman ship. They would tell immediately when there was a weakness in the wagon train defense. The shrill command would then be given and the braves would enter the inside of the circle at the weak point, from there they would systematically annihilate every living person in the camp, just as they had twice done before.

There was a lot of nervous frightened activity among the people of the wagon train. Billy, knowing the young men's accuracy, assigned one every third wagon, giving each one sixteen cartridges, telling them to make dead sure of their accuracy. Milly Dreher and Hilda Heilman were busy keeping the ladies and children as calm as could be expected, but they took note of what

Billy was doing. The same could be said of Ben Thompson and Glen Forester, and there were others who saw the swiftness of Billy's actions. In the time of extreme crisis for families and individuals, Billy's action and manner of command could not be forgotten.

Shortly after first light, the Indians came sweeping down expecting to catch their prey unaware, expecting to find the wagons lined for travel. At one hundred yards Billy fired, A big brave on a large red stallion immediately dropped. From then on, the air was full of the smell of gunpowder. Billy was able to detect multiple Henry shots in addition to his own. Finally, the Indians withdrew more than one hundred yards up on a hill overlooking the camp. But not before Billy noticed the Natives number had been cut, in fact of the thirty there were fifteen left.

There was a slight lull in the shooting when three wagons down, Billy heard the sharp crack of Jimmy's rifle. On the hill a brave on a fine horse slowly fell from his horse. For Three Bears, this was the deciding factor. It was too costly. He had planned on a surprise attack on an unsuspecting wagon train, only to discover the exact opposite. They might have taken the loss of one of their braves at one hundred yards seriously at the beginning, but they thought they would still be victors. But they sought in vain to discover a weak spot in the surrounding area of the wagon train defense and this coupled with something they had never experienced before. There was a distinct crack of a rifle they have never experienced before. It was steady and extremely accurate. There was no reloading between shots. And the worst of all for the natives, it was well placed around the circle of the wagons. There simply was no weakness.

When Jimmy dropped the brave at an incredible 150 yards, it was the deciding factor. Three Bears was forced to withdraw. He and his braves would never again attack a wagon train. There was a terrible sadness with their return to the Indian encampment. The missing Braves would leave squares and children without food and care.

One of the returning younger warriors had listened carefully to Three Bears account of the battle. He took note of Three Bears description of the tall young white eyes with a red shirt who according to Three Bears, was responsible for their losses.

Three Bears had seen Red Shirt before coming out of the land they were driven out of. Their paths had crossed north of

Dyersburg, Tennessee on the day the Indian removal had been enforced. Red shirt was also observed game hunting for the wagon train. He was the one who spearheaded the attack on the Braves. Three Bears knew Billy was vitally connected with their defeat. Out of Three Bear's bitter anguish he said young Red Shirt should pay for it. The young brave had listened with the intent to do just as Three Bears said. Meanwhile their situation was desperate. They had depended upon the wagon train for their food. The wagon people's cattle would keep them for some time, now they were without.

Ben Thompson's wagon train had not escaped unscathed. They were fortunate in one regard. There had been no loss of life, but there was some seriously wounded. Of the wounded, wagon train master Ben Thompson had the most serious wound taking an arrow in the left shoulder resulting in a considerable loss of blood and leaving him in a weakened condition. The next two men in command likewise had serious wounds and would be unable to drive their schooners or do anything for some time. Momentarily it left the camp in disarray. It was imperative without any delay that the remaining men of the wagon train hold council.

They had just finished the battle and the entire wagon continuance of wagon folk stood in the wagon circle. They begin to cast looks back and forth as to who lead the wagon train. This was a critical point for the entire camp. Their future would rest in the hands of their choice. They were shaking from what they had just come through. Some of the more intelligent had been alarmed so deeply by the site of the Warriors sweeping down on them, they had good reason to believe their end was near. They were paralyzed by fear, but something had to be done.

Without hesitation, Milly Dreher, who's intelligence and sound judgment was highly respected among the wagon folk, spoke out in a strong clear voice.

"Ben's responsibility could temporarily be shared by three." But before Milly could add any more, Jake Heilman jumped in front of Milly and in a loud shrill unkind voice said "Shut your mouth. The men would manage the situation." Thinking he had done something brave he looked around for approval. Mr. and Mrs. Heilman were deeply ashamed and embarrassed by Jake's words and actions. But before anyone knew what was happening Billy, was standing before Jake. He landed a short right upper cut right to Jake's jaw.

The men folk talked later of seeing six inches of daylight under Jakes feet from the blow. When Jake came down, he staggered backward ten feet before lighting on the seat of his pants. Billy was right on him, looking down at Jake, in a strong clear voice Billy said, "Men don't treat women folk like that."

There was a dead silence among the wagon folk, except for two audible snickers coming from the back of the wagon where Glen Forester was standing next to Ben Thompson, who was lying inside.

Jake then made the wisest decision thus far in his young life, he stayed on his backside. For Jake it was the beginning of becoming a real man, for which his parents would be forever grateful and proud.

Milly, seeing no need to waste time continued her words with a Proverb of old, "the threefold cord is not easily broken." The bulk of the wagon train were God-fearing people, and they recognize the proverb. They leaned forward to hear the rest of Milly's speech. Milly continued, "Herb Jenkins would be in charge of judgement matters." This struck a fine note with all, Herb was wise and his sure judgment everyone agreed upon.

Next, Milly suggested someone oversee to make sure all had adequate food. To this there was several women who stepped forward. One said, "Milly Dreher would be more than adequate for the task." Many applauded, and Milly blushed while several seconded her nomination. Again, there was staunch support from the small crowd.

"The third choice and most difficult," Milly said, "would be that of leading the wagons and most important of all, providing protection in case of further trouble." She then paused for a moment and remarked that, "despite his age of only eighteen years, he had already shown remarkable leadership ability in his marksmanship and his wisdom in deploying the other young men to strategic positions in protecting the wagon train. He had displayed a distinctive quality of leadership in a moment of terror." Milly continued her remarks, "Billy knew what had to be done and he did it." Milly clearly stated to the wagon folk what Billy had just accomplished, and it brought forth a moment of gratitude from men, women and children of the wagon train. There were hankies brought forth by several of the women.

Milly was not the only one knowing what Billy had meant to their safety less than an hour before. Milly had barely finished when there was a huge deafening spontaneous ovation. Billy was so stricken he dropped his head, and the noise grew louder. Billy turned and motioned Jimmy, Isaiah, Melvin, and Jeremy to come forward, only to cause the noise to continue. When quiet was restored, their business was complete. The parents of the boys were so moved there were handkerchiefs a plenty.

Billy then spoke in a loud, clear, commanding tone, "Folks, we need to be on the move." Billy then gave the four boys an immediate task. They were to remove the strewn Indian bodies to the hill where Three Bears was last seen and place them in a decent row. This deeply touched the wagon people. In less than a half hour the wagons were lined up and Billy gave the command, "Wagons ho!"

With Billy's command there was a collective feeling of security among the wagon train constituency. It was a solitary conviction of their wise choice of the interim leadership. More than that there was a conviction of the future success of their mission. It would be accomplished with relief and happiness despite the awareness of future difficulties they were sure to encounter.

They had placed their confidence in Billy, and they would not be disappointed.

A week afterward Jake's jaw was still sore. He had been solitary for the entire week, noticeably to his parents. Partly because of a sore jaw, but more so because he had done some serious thinking which was new for Jake. Jake had made an agonizing reappraisal of his words spoken to Milly Dreher, and of his general attitude about himself and other people. Jake had a sense of shame when he saw the direction he was taking. Mr. and Mrs. Heilman knew he was meditating seriously on something but were unable to comprehend what it would be. Frankly, they were worried what was going on in Jake's mind.

On the eve of a long day of travel a week after the wagon train meeting, Jake spoke up to his parents at the evening meal. He said he had something to say to them. With some consternation, they noted he was struggling to put his words together. He finally blurted it out. "I want to make some changes in my life." It was a wholehearted confession of a young man sorry for what he had done to other people, and his parents. He vowed to change his general attitude. His parents were spellbound silent. He continued by asking them a question, "Do you think it would be all right if I apologized to Mrs. Dreher." Unable to speak they nodded their heads.

With this Jake went directly to the Dreher wagon. Martha broke down in tears. While holding Martha in his arms John Heilman spoke softly in her ear, "Martha our boy will be a man after all."

Ben Thompson and Glen Forester had observed the wagon train meeting. Glen was next to Ben stretched out in a wagon bed. With Billy's age and all, Ben was understandably concerned about the leadership Billy would provide. Glen accurately pointed out to Ben there simply was no one else. They witnessed the wagon train meeting. They heard every word and shared in the ovation of Billy's election.

Billy made a habit of confiding in Ben and Glen in wagon train decisions. He valued the older men's knowledge and opinions. In fact, they had discussed Billy at length before Ben's earlier selection.

Glen said, "Billy and another lad named Jimmy each had an accurate sense of awareness of situations around them and would make them more than a meat provider on daily hunting trips." When Ben's Scout had declined a trip at the last minute of departure, leaving Ben with the later selection task. Billy and Jimmy had more than fit the task.

Glen overheard a discussion among the lady folk of the wagon train considering the way young Jake had been taken a liking to Billy after the blow on the jaw. Jake had done a complete turnaround with his attitude about himself and people. His apology to Milly Dreher was recorded by all who heard. Martha Heilman had often cried herself asleep in worry over the direction Jake was pursuing. Martha was reported to have said, I'm grateful beyond measure for the influence Billy has on Jake." Glen related Billy's good influence on Ben in the simplest of words, "He makes wayward men better."

Billy wasted no time assigning duties. "Jimmy, you and Isaiah are in charge of daily hunting and scouting responsibilities." Billy knew he would not have to explain scouting responsibilities to them. They knew what had to be done and they would do it. "Melvin and Jeremy, you will drive the wagons for the two wounded men."

Jake Heilman saw this but was not put out because he was overlooked. Since Jake's change of mind, he had thought much of Billy and all he meant to the wagon train. He had concluded that Billy was all right and had something special about him. Jake spoke to his mother, "I want to be friends with Billy." Martha answered, "Jake Heilman, if you bide your time, your chance may come." Martha did not know she spoke prophetically.

Milly Dreher had told Billy of Jake's visit and the sincerity of his words. She had been shocked at his approach to their wagon. However, when Jake disclosed the full intent of his mission, Milly had to brush away a tear. She sent Jake home with a large piece of apple pie, two pieces in fact. One of them was

Billy's, Billy just laughed and thought well of Jake.

Billy would spend the next three weeks hard in the saddle. However, he made it a point to be in daily contact with Wagon Master Ben Thompson and keeping him well informed. Glen was always present except for when busy. The older experienced man took note of when there was a good, better, or best decision to be made, the best was always chosen. Ben commented to Glen, "The majority of men would not even have thought of the other possibilities."

One late afternoon, while conversing, Ben spoke in a solemn manner, "Glen, I am worried about the boy after the Idaho break." "I have been thinking the same," answered Glen. No more was said, but Glen had been thinking it over and knew what he would do. From there on every occasion, Glen told Billy everything he remembered about crossing Nevada and on to California. It would be a long hard dangerous journey. But with what Glen and Andrew Winstead had given he would be ready for it. Glen had made it a point to lay out the minute things of the trail each day. Billy was attentive, he could read between the lines, able to see into what he was being told.

Meanwhile the Indian's plight had worsened. Most noticeably in the small children. Their skin was pale, their bellies were swollen, their cries were heard throughout the camp. The small number of braves were unable to supply enough food for all. There was hunger on every side. Something had to be done.

Three Bears had thought much and had at last formulated his plan. The bodies of the braves had been left knowing he would return for them. The way they were left made Three Bears think on the wagon people's disposition.

He turned to his friend, Lone Eagle. "Our people are starving. Red Shirt will help us." Lone Eagle replied, "Red Shirt is one to watch. But I believe you are right. He will help us." For some innate reason Three Bears knew Red Shirt was responsible and reasoned that Red Shirt would not let his people go hungry. He must go with three of his braves to the wagon people for food.

Three Bears and his Braves were approaching the moving wagon train and had stopped a short distance of two hundred yards, not knowing the exact responses of people they were approaching.

They were not coming unaware. Jimmy and Isaiah had spotted their presence long before. Billy, Ben, and Glen had discussed the situation. Billy had guessed why they were coming but could not take any chances. Billy, Glen, and Jimmy would meet with the Indians. Glen knew some Choctaw and would carry the conversation.

Once ready to leave, Billy noted Jake Heilman standing nearby. Of late Billy had been aware of Jake's presence whenever there was something needed to be done. It was a tense moment, Billy spoke in a clear voice, "Jake, come with us." Jake was on his horse immediately following the other three.

Earlier that morning Isaiah and Jimmy had brought down three antilope. Billy had informed Isaiah to stand ready with the three antelope on a pack horse. When and if Billy gave the command, Isaiah was to bring them out to the meeting.

It was a tense moment as they rode up to the natives. Three Bears stood to the foreground. Glen initiated the meeting with a peace sign. Three Bears quickly followed with the same. The thin faces and hollow eye sockets convinced Billy he had guessed correctly. They were starving. Glen and Three Bears conversed back and forth, and shortly Glen turned to Billy saying, "They need food." Billy spoke clearly to Glen, "Tell them we will give them food." All the Braves relaxed except one. Billy signaled to Isaiah who quickly rode to the meeting with the three antelope on the pack horse. The expression in the eyes of Three Bears conveyed to Billy his gratitude.

Three Bears then rode directly up to Billy. Glen told Ben later, "Most men would have reacted. Billy never flinched, he stood tall in the saddle." Three Bears took a rawhide with a beautiful turquoise stone attached from his neck and presented it to the young man who had defeated him in battle but had shown respect for his dead warriors and was now giving his people and his children food when they needed it. Billy knew it was a beautiful and rare gift, he also knew he could not refuse the gift. Billy received the gift with a slight nod of approval. Three Bears fully recognized Billy's sincerity.

With that there was a sense of closure. Billy was about to give the reins of the pack horse to Three Bears, when Jimmy saw a young brave behind the Indian group had raised his bow with dead aim at Billy. It happened too quickly; Jimmy had no time to react. Then there was a deafening shot as the young native dropped listlessly to the ground. Everyone in the meeting knew his aim was for Billy, including Billy. Smoke was still showing from Jake's .45. Everyone knew where the shot came from. Jake had seen the ugly look on the young brave's face and the way his bow was across his lap for use. Jake's alertness saved Billy's life.

Three Bears and the remaining Braves were paralyzed. Billy, as though nothing had happened, gave the pack horse reigns to Three Bears. Lone Eagle, one of the other braves, bound the fallen brave to his horse. Three Bears and the group turned and left. Three Bears and his people ate well that evening. The little children were playing, the women and the Warriors were able to sleep. The next morning the pack horse was found staked outside of the wagon circle.

It was known all over camp what Jake had done. Later, without a word spoken, Billy would walk up to Jake and extend his hand. Neither spoke. Jake knew Billy's gratitude.

Someone else would notice Jake. The Robins family's oldest daughter, Mary Lou, was quite attractive. Jake had looked her way several times before.

Mary Lou had seen Jake's attention, but she was turned off by his rude disposition and sour attitude. She did what all young ladies do in a like situation, she looked the other way. Jake had not forgotten Mary Lou, he just concluded he had no chance. Jake had seen Mary Lou's reluctance and knew what it meant.

Because of Jake's turnaround and what he had done for Billy, there was a change in Mary Lou. Shortly after the Robins family invited the Heilman family over for an evening meal. Before the wagon train reached the California Oregon divide Judge elect, Herb Jenkins, performed a wedding ceremony, Billy was best man.

Their contact with Three Bears occurred once more. The reduced number of braves meant there was not enough food to go around. Three Bears had done the only thing he could do. He traveled several miles behind the wagon train hoping for a scraps and help. Jimmy and Isaiah saw what the Natives were doing and reported it to Billy. Billy told Jimmy and Isaiah to seek for a way to help the natives.

While hunting two days later, Jimmy and Isaiah came across four stray buffalo. The natives also saw the four buffalo, but by now they had eaten all their horses and were unable, after numerous attempts, to get within bow range. At 150 yards, well beyond the normal range of their Henry's, Jimmy and Isaiah picked off two Buffalo. Three Bears and five of his best warriors stood at a distance not knowing what to do. Jimmy gave a clear command, waving them to the downed Buffalo. Jimmy only had to wave once. The Braves moved quickly. There would be enough to eat in the Indian camp for some time.

That evening around the fire, Three Bears asked his men how they could repay the white eyes. Lone Eagle spoke out, "I will pledge if ever I have the chance, I will protect them on their journey, even to my death." Lone Eagle did not know the future, but he gave the pledge in a manner that everyone knew he would do it. For the Indians, the question was resolved. It would never be discussed again.

The presence of the larger native group following Three Bears had not gone undetected. Jimmy and Isaiah had extended their hunting range beyond Three Bears. They had discovered the larger body of natives and reported to Billy.

Billy, Ben, and Glen had discussed the situation regarding the imminent danger to the wagon train. The detailed accuracy of the report Jimmy and Isaiah gave was not comforting to Ben. Glen listened carefully to Billy's assessment of what they faced. Billy commented, "Three Bears and Lone Eagle are proud men. They will join us if there is an attack. The other group will not want this."

Three days later Three Bears and his people met the larger band of Choctaw warriors who had been tracking the wagon train for attack. They had picked up Three Bear's track and wanted to know why they were tracking the wagon train with such a small number of warriors, and no horses. When they received the full story, they were deeply moved. After Three Bears told them of the repeating rifles and their accuracy, the Choctaw band decided to discontinue their tracking. They also noted the disapproval of their proposed attack by one brave in particular, Lone Eagle. Lone Eagle was known among the Choctaw people. He was a fearless warrior who would fight to the death. Warriors from the new band had heard of Lone Eagle's pledge and they knew the consequences of contending with Lone Eagle. The result was Three Bears, and his people would not need Red Shirt's help again. They joined forces with the other Choctaw and departed another way. It was commonly agreed knowledge among the Choctaw there would be no more attacks on Red Shirt's wagon train. It would be so.

Ben and Glen had told Billy of a river they would soon have to cross. It was later known as the South Platte, and it could be extremely dangerous, depending upon the rains. As the wagon train approached the river, Billy fully understood their concerns. The river had wildly exceeded in its banks. It was tumultuous in its roar. Billy had selected a crossing five miles further upstream, not pinched and not so violent in its passage. He had studied the waters on a river on the farm and knew how to read the depths of the waters and its current. More than once he had to pull cattle from the deep water.

Mr. Robins argued the additional five miles of travel would take extra time. Mr. Robins said it would tire already tired animals that needed rest He challenged Billy by saying there was no real danger and he would prove his point by crossing the stream himself. Billy tried in vain to change Mr. Robin's mind, But Robins was determined. Billy could do nothing, but station Jimmy and Isaiah downstream with lariats. Robins and his team were halfway across, some thinking he might make it, when the wagon capsized and was swept uncontrollably downstream. Some real swift and intelligent moves by Jimmy and Isaiah brought Mr. Robins, the team, and a damaged wagon to shore.

Mrs. Robins, who refused to ride the river with her husband, stood weeping and wondering what they would do the rest of the trip. Not for long, Martha Heilman was at her side instantly taking her in her arms. They would find room for them until Glen had repaired the wagon.

The wheels and frame were still intact, Glen fixed it without loss of time. Billy wondered how he did it while on the road. Five miles further upstream with Billy's direction the entire train crossed the South Platte without difficulty.

Ben Thompson's wagon train reached Fort Hall Idaho in the latter part of July after spending over three months on the trail. Ben wanted to give Billy a resounding farewell with Billy's departure from his wagon train, but Billy refused. Billy was not much for attention and besides, he was anxious to join the California wagon train. Billy took particular care and thanking the Dreher's and in bidding farewell to the four young men and Jake Heilman all of whom he had grown quite fond.

Early the next morning Glen Forester would not miss seeing Billy off and was present when Billy left. Billy and Arkie were packed and ready when Glen appeared next to Billy, "Billy when you get to Donner's Pass, it's a mite bit cold up there at night. I want you to have this. It will keep you warm on a frosty night." It was a buffalo robe of some value and Billy was reluctant to take it. Glen insisted, saying, "Billy, I know you will need it." Billy took it and for some unknown reason he knew it would play an important part in his future. After thanking Glen, Billy mounted Arkie and road silently southwest on the California trail.

Glen lingered a little while longer and brushing the mist from his eyes, he thought he would never see the lad again. It brought a sadness to Glen; he had never had a family. He left a small Missouri town forty-five years ago when he was fifteen years old. He was an orphan picked up at twelve years old by a farmer who every day made him do a man's work and then some. After three long hard years Glen decided to leave. Late one evening, he made his way to Independence, Missouri. He apprenticed with a blacksmith where he learned the trade, and he had learned his trade well. Five years later at the age of twenty a wagon train headed West, due to a last-minute cancellation, they needed a good horseman. Glen took the job. In subsequent years he made four trips from independence Missouri to the West: three to California and one to Oregon.

He had been through more than one Indian raid and had been left for dead on one, only to be found a week later by another wagon train. No one ever knew how he had survived. Some old timers claimed he had more than one life. The fifth and final trip was to be with Ben Thompson to Oregon.

Seeing Billy for the last time caused Glen to do some reflection. He was musing over the past four months. He was thinking of all the time spent sharing his wagon train knowledge with Billy, and of all the trying times he had stood with Billy, when Glen suddenly realized there would always be a place in his heart for Billy. In future days he would wonder and yes, he would worry how Billy was, how he was doing and if he made it to

Sacramento. Then Glen realized something he had never felt before. Billy was more than an acquaintance. Glen's concern for Billy had given them a different relationship, Glen had felt responsible for Billy. Glen had never experienced the word family. Suddenly it dawned on Glen, Billy was like family and Glen knew what parting was like.

PART II

TWO YOUNG PEOPLE

Betty Jane Watson and Rodney Hartford had met when she was fourteen and he was sixteen. They met at a family get together in Boston. He was very handsome, so much so that all the young ladies wanted him. Betty Jane was completely taken by Rodney. Later he and his parents had successfully taken a wagon train to Californiaand he had written three times to her. He wanted her to come to California and they would be married. Betty Jane's parents did not want her to go. Betty Jane had a strange feeling that California was her destiny.

Howard and Kate Johnson, longtime friends of the Watson family, had written to a friend, John Matson, who was a Wagon Master. Matson informed them he was heading a wagon train from Independence, Missouri to Sacramento, California in April. The Johnsons had written back to Matson informing him of their wish to travel with the California train. Betty Jane and her family had heard from the Johnsons, and at her insistence, her mother and father had finally conceded, chiefly because she would be traveling with the Johnsons. Betty Jane was not a headstrong person, but she was determined to go west. A week later after the California train had left Independence, Missouri, Glen Forester had mentioned seeing a beautiful girl leave on the California train. Betty Jane was on the California train.

After departing from Fort Hall, Billy and Arkie followed the California trail. Shortly after they reached the Raft River on the very tip of Northwest Nevada and were traveling in a southwesterly direction toward what is now known as Wells. Unbeknownst to Billy the California wagon train he sought to catch had encountered difficulty two days in succession. Two wagons demanded repair and were unable to travel because of breakage. Wagon master John Matson elected to wait and repair rather than force the repaired wagons to catch up.

It would take Billy five days to catch up to the California train. But Billy began picking up some troubling signs the minute he left the Raft River. There was an excessive number of unshod marks of mustangs. These marks sent a chill up Billy's spine. Billy turned to Arkie, "Arkie there's trouble ahead." Arkie look at Billy and snorted.

Blended in with the mustang tracks were two shod horses, one with a strange mark on the right front hoof. Billy had seen the same mark on a track before leaving Independence, Missouri, and again at Fort Hall. The track had been old, but it was unmistakably a match to the fresh one Billy was now seeing.

It was late afternoon on the fifth day when Billy came over a rise seeing a sight his eyes wished they had never seen. The wagon train had been annihilated. The ground was red with blood, bodies were strewn everywhere. Billy stomach wrenched within him. He knew he dare not stay in the vicinity. He crossed over the creek both he and the wagon trail had followed.

Billy turned in his saddle for one more look before leaving. He knew he could not stay and care for the dead. As he looked at the bodies of men, women, and children he wondered what kind of people could do such a thing.

There was a huge tree on the edge of the creek. The spring waters had eroded the bank and exposed some of its roots. Archie snorted at something. When Billy turned, a figure staggered out of the water in front of him. Billy was off Arkie in an instant and then he saw it was a young lady. She was terribly cold. When she looked up and saw him, she panicked. Billy could see she was frightened and nearly froze. But when he looked into her eyes, he momentarily had a strange sensation that he did not understand. They were the most beautiful eyes he had ever seen.

He spoke in a clear steady voice, "We can't stay here." Reaching in his saddle bag he pulled out a pair of his trousers and a flannel shirt, "Go on the other side of Arkie and put these on. We have got to get out of here." She knew Arkie must be the horse and she did not know why, but she did exactly as she was told. In no time at all she appeared from the other side of the horse. She was so cold she was trembling violently. He had a large buffalo robe he put around her. Then he picked her up and sat her on the back of the horse behind the saddle and he was in the saddle, and they were moving.

He spoke once more, "You will have to hang on to me." Once again, she did what she was told to do, and once again she did not know why. Putting her arms around his waist she felt the shape of his body realizing there was no excess. She was five feet, six inches tall, and weighed 115 pounds. He picked her up like a feather and put her on his horse. At his command Arkie began to trot in a steady gait.

The sun disappeared. They kept riding. Finally, after a good three hours they were among a small grove of trees. They came to halt, but long before the buffalo robe brought warmth to her body. She stopped trembling. In fact, the trauma she had gone through and the shock of the freezing water she had been in for three hours, left her so fatigued she almost went to sleep.

He stepped down off the horse and lifted her to the ground. In a brief time, he had a fire going, and handing her a strip of dried venison, he said, "all we got this evening." Shortly after, he said "You sleep in the robe." She knew he wanted her to sleep so she wrapped up in the robe and did just that.

When she woke the sun was up and he had a fire with two medium size bass frying in a small pan. It looked funny to her, the heads were sticking out one side of the pan and their tails out the other. It was obvious to her he did not know how to cook. She spoke for the first time, "I have to wash." He looked at her and nodded.

While traveling last night, they had never left the creek. It was the same one the wagon train had traveled by. She turned and walked to the creek making sure he could not see her. After washing and dressing she returned to where he was. As she approached him, he turned looking directly at her. He abruptly stopped what he was doing. Billy had never looked at a girl before. He had seen girls in Dyersburg, but never really looked.

Her hair was jet black, her complexion was exceptionally light with slight rosy cheeks, her lips were red. Her eyes were blue so far beyond beautiful. Billy had never seen anything like them before. Billy again had the strange sensation when he looked into her eyes that he had the day before.

She had been looked at since she was thirteen years old. She had seen every kind of a look in the book, but never had she seen one like this. She was momentarily frightened. She blurted out, "I am promised to someone in California." Unable to think why she said it, she was totally embarrassed. He just looked at her and commented, "I'm happy for you." and followed with, "What is your name?" She looked at him realizing they did not even know each other's names and responded, "I'm Betty Jane Watson, and your name?" he answered "William McGovern, I go by 'Billy.' Nice to know you ma'am."

Shortly after he asked her a direct question, "Do you know how to use a revolver?" After thinking momentarily why he would ask such a question, she answered, "Yes, I do, why do you ask?"

Billy spoke clearly, "In the saddle pack on the back of my saddle I put a gun." He never said anymore. But it was the Colt .45 given to Billy on the eve their departure from Independence. He then offered her a fish for breakfast which she ate heartily.

But her mind was busy sizing up Billy. Betty Jane was not a proud young lady, and neither was she foolish. She was clever and very perceptive, always alert because with her looks she had to be. She noticed he was about six foot two or three and weighed 180 some odd pounds. His hair was thick and sandy colored, his eyes were dark blue. Betty Jane thought him to be rugged and not very handsome, certainly not in the same class as Rodney Hartford, her fiancé in California. After seeing his awkwardness in cooking, she had thought him to be a farm boy. Billy was not a person of many words he only spoke to her when necessary. Because of this Betty Jane thought he lacked intelligence. Yet there was something about him she could not place with other young men she had met, and she never bothered to ask herself what it was.

She would find out later she had completely miscalculated him. It would be almost impossible to change the groundwork she was setting. It would be one of the most painful experiences Betty Jane would ever face. It would take a real lady and every bit of a woman. The consequence of Betty Jane's thinking and her action toward Billy would haunt her. The pain would be magnified because it was her thinking. She had not allowed herself to think anything other than her future with Rodney Hartford

Billy and Betty Jane did not know they were being tracked for attack by two men. Zedekiah and Colby Benson were brothers quite different in physical appearance only.

Zedekiah the oldest, was small and snake like in looks. He had a dark complexion and stringy, greasy black hair. But his giveaway feature was the hideous, deranged look on his face. It became more pronounced when he looked upon women and children. More than once his mere gaze had left a young lady or a little child in utter in fright. From this, Zedekiah received a strange, exhilarating, and uncontrollable passion.

At this point Zedekiah became a killer. He used gun or knife; he favored the knife.

Betty Jane had seen Zedekiah and Colby twice before. They had been at Independence, Missouri and at Fort Hall. She had been keenly aware of Zedekiah's gazing attention. She had come to two conclusions; Zedekiah was deeply deranged and secondly, she would be in definite danger if ever in his presence.

Colby stood six foot four inches, weighed about 250 pounds, and was unusually strong in his forearms. He had a light chalk-like complexion with nondescript light grey eyes. His personality was much the same as

Zedekiah, except for one propensity: He was a killer who crushed his victims. He loved the sound of snapping bones when he applied pressure to his victim's chest area. Once in his grasp no one had ever escaped.

In a more contemporary society Zedekiah and Colby would both have resided in an asylum. Which would have been healing for both them and society. But in their time such places were limited. Such was the old west

The two men did not know they also were being tracked and watched. A lone rider had been following Billy ever since he left the Oregon wagon train at Fort

Hall. The rider had seen two men looking around the wagon train massacre where Billy had picked up the girl. The lone Rider surmise they were wicked white men, and we are looking for something or someone they wanted badly. He was a Choctaw brave who had seen white eyes men like them before. The two men had looked carefully and seen the girls tracks to Billy's horse. The Choctaw then knew what they wanted. They wanted the girl. He knew they would kill Billy and the girl also.

The two men in pursuit, Zedekiah and Colby Benson were Texans. They were ruthless young men without scruples.

Zedekiah had seen Betty Jane at Independence, Missouri, and Fort Hall in Idaho. He knew she was on the California wagon train. He and Colby worked with the band of Indian renegades made up of disgruntled natives from the removal acts.

Zedekiah and Colby spent time around the various trading posts waiting for a wagon train to pass through. After thoroughly looking over the train they then reported to the band of renegade natives what they had seen. An attack would be planned and conducted. Twice before the plan had worked. It was a dirty low-down business. Few could stomach it. Zedekiah and Colby found delight in it.

Jay Benson, their father, had been part of "the bushwhackers" led by William Clark Quantrill. Quantrill, a Confederate guerilla leader during the Civil War, was responsible for some terrible atrocities against men, women, and children. Jay Benson had often related the terror they had inflicted upon the unprotected Union settlements. Jay's two sons had listened to their father's stories, and how he told them. Zedekiah had exceeded his father's evil deranged disposition. Betty Jane had seen both Zedekiah and Colby take part with the braves on the day of the California wagon train massacre. She witnessed Zedekiah's acts. Zedekiah particularly liked to torture women and little children. Betty Jane could not talk or think about what she had seen.

This time there were two groups of settlers passing Fort Hall. The first would go to California and the second, coming a week later, would go on to Oregon. Zedekiah and Colby reported the California group only to the natives. They had reason; Zedekiah wanted the girl.

It was mid-morning, Billy stopped and let Arkie drink, he and Betty Jane were to stretch their muscles and relax a moment. Billy had stepped down from Arkie when suddenly there was a gunshot. He turned seeing a huge man falling at his feet; Betty Janes revolver was just hitting the ground with smoke emitting from the barrel. An ugly little man had slapped Betty Jane knocking the revolver to the ground. He had grabbed Arkie's reins leading Arkie and Betty Jane away at an in creditable speed. Billy snatched the gun off the ground, but could not risk shooting Betty Jane, who was between him and the rider. If he whistled, Arkie would immediately stop and throw Betty Jane. He could not see the big man's horse as it was behind some bushes, and he had no timely way of tracking Arkie. Billy did not understand why but the thought of losing the girl hit him hard. Arkie would be a terrible loss, but the loss of Betty Jane was greater. Later Billy would think about it and wonder why he felt as he did.

Just then he heard a shot coming from the direction Betty Jane and Arkie had gone. He was looking frantically for the big man's horse when he saw a slumped rider coming stringing a pair of horses. The second horse was Arkie, with Betty Jane in the saddle. The slumped lead rider was not recognizable at first. As they came closer, he realized it was Lone Eagle. Billy could not make out what had taken place, but he could see Lone Eagle was severely wounded. Betty Jane looked ready to collapse but did not appear to be wounded. Arkie looked at Billy and took a drink.

Billy lowered Lone Eagle from the mustang's back and laid the brave and Betty Jane under the shade of the tree. Betty Jane was sure Billy never saw what took place with the big man. She would tell him the full story later, now was not the time, Lone Eagle was dying. Betty Jane watched Billy tend to Lone Eagle like he would his child. She would never forget it. Later it would come to her memory.

Lone Eagle had a gut shot wound; it was the worst way to go. Billy wrapped a shirt around Lone Eagles middle tying it tightly. Lone Eagles eyes showed the pain, but he uttered not a sound. Lone Eagle glanced upwardly; Billy knew instantly what he wanted. Billy cut four poles seven feet long with a diameter of two inches. Each pole was shaped round at the top. Billy took rawhide from Lone Eagle jacket and trousers. Billy was building a burial platform for a Lone Eagle and Lone Eagle knew it. The platform would have a top surface of three by seven feet. Lone Eagle would take his rest upon a strongly built wooded surface.

Lone Eagle was passing this world to the next triumphantly, he had paid the debt as he told his people he would do. Billy knew at that moment Lone Eagle had entered the place Indians call the happy hunting ground. When Lone Eagle's life left him, Billy put him on the burial platform. For Lone Eagle life was finished, he had kept his word to his people. Lone Eagle's life was over, Billy's was only beginning.

When Lone Eagle was dying, he struggled to tell Billy something. Billy finally got the gist of Lone Eagle's words. Lone Eagle wanted Betty Jane to have his horse, and the horse had a name.

When Billy finally understood he spoke to Betty Jane. "He wants you to have his horse, Lightning." Betty Jane looked down at Lone Eagle and burst into tears. Lone Eagle had just saved her life and now he was giving her the only thing he had. Lone Eagle saw the look in Betty Janes eyes, it was a moment of triumph for Lone Eagle.

As he was taking his last breath, Lone Eagle spoke to Billy and Betty Jane one last time. He used a Choctaw word they did not understand, and he was addressing both of them. Both Billy and Betty Jane knew what Lone Eagle had done for them. Much later Billy and Betty

Jane would be told the meaning of the word.

Billy never knew Zedekiah and Colby Benson, but despite all that had taken place, Billy gave them a proper burial, a good distance away from Lone Eagle. They belong to someone someplace. Billy was right, a mother would never see her boys again.

Billy was aware it had been a long and traumatic day for Betty Jane. He elected not to try and move a few more miles. They would wait and start early next morning, and it would give him ample time to look at the added horses the remaining part of the day.

Billy took a long look at the mustang stallion, and he saw what a beautiful animal it was. The horse was highly intelligent, older than Arkie and, more important, the horse did not have the typical rough nature of a Mustang. Lightning was mild mannered which made him an excellent horse for Betty Jane.

The Benson horses were slightly larger than Arkie or Lightning. They were well paired and had seen many miles. Billy could use them as light packhorses, or even ride them on occasion to provide Arkie and Lightning some sorely needed rest.

Billy took the saddle from the small horse Lone Eagle had returned with and walked to where Lightning was feeding. Betty Jane would need a saddle and he wondered how the horse would react to something he was not used to. Lightning was contently munching a nice patch of grass when Billy approached him with a blanket. The horse kept on eating when it was put in place, which was what he expected. Then Billy gently put the saddle on Lightning's back. Lighting turned and looked at Billy, continuing munching. It caused Billy to conclude it was not the first time Lightening wore a saddle.

Betty Jane had thoughtfully watched Billy and Lightning while it was transpiring. She could not help noticing Billy's action, and Lightning's reaction. She understood what Billy was doing, she would need a saddle. She had never ridden without one. Betty Jane was not a person to stand idly. She suggested to Billy she do the cooking. Billy had agreed, not saying anything about how happy it made him. For two reasons, he did not like to cook and secondly it was she was taking a hand in daily chores. He found out later there was a third reason the transfer of cooking responsibility was a wise decision; Betty Jane could cook.

She did something else, she went through the contents stashed on the three of the other horses. Billy saw what she was doing what he had planned to do. Billy again noted she was taking a part in what was going to be a long hard journey.

Betty Jane looked over Lone Eagle's possessions first. There was hardly anything there. His bow, a handful of arrows, and a few strips of buffalo and antelope jerky was all Betty Jane found. She did not how he could survive on so little. She asked Billy later what Lone Eagle was doing out traveling alone with nothing to keep him. Billy had looked down and in a soft voice he said, "He was paying a debt."

On Zedekiah's horse there was little of value except for three items: the revolver he had used to shoot Lone Eagle, old pieces of clothing, and a large knife she had seen him use during the raid. When she saw the knife, she was so traumatized she started to collapse. Billy saw her and caught her before she fell. He knew there was something about that knife that caused Betty Jane to faint.

Colby's horse was stocked differently. Betty Jane found usable items in the two small front bags – a knife, compass, small map, pencil and notebook, and canteen. The larger saddle pack had two large bags, one on each side of the horse, and contained both cooking utensils and provisions. A large bedroll was strapped on top of the pack. Colby had obviously been the cook. The saddle pack was heavy, but back east, Betty Jane had been raised on a farm near Boston. She had no problem unloading the pack.

Among the contents of the big man's sack, she found a large cast iron skillet frying pan which made her smile, when she thought of Billy frying the fish. There was also a cup, a saucepan, and two forks. Lastly, she came to some items Billy never carried. There was a sack of flour, some dried apples, a small amount of sugar and salt and what Betty Jane treasured most, some beans. His blanket, like Zedekiah's, could be used if washed.

On the very bottom of Colby's bag, she found another revolver. Betty June wondered why most western men wore their revolvers and Colby had other means of killing men which he enjoyed more. Betty Jane had seen him crush two helpless unsuspecting men on the day of the massacre. When she realized how close Colby was to unaware Billy, she moved quickly, and she knew what she was doing. Her shot hit Colby in the temple.

The next morning Betty Jane told Billy of the attack on the wagon train. It was not easy for her to do so. She had to stop four or five times, each time breaking down with tears. Billy did not know why, but each time she broke down he wanted to take her in his arms. He knew it was not the thing to do, and he was right.

She told of seeing the two men at Independence, Missouri, and again at Fort Hall in Idaho. Each time the smaller one with the ugly deranged look was constantly starring at her. On the day of the Indian raid, they were there, taking part in the massacre. Then she began to sob so violently her whole body trembled. Something about Zedekiah made her lose control. It took every ounce of man in Billy to keep from taking her in his arms.

She then told Billy how she had escaped death during the raid. "I was traveling with the Johnsons, friends of my parents, back in Boston. The evening before, the wagons were parked in their usual circle pattern. And by chance our wagon was parked next to the large tree on the creek. Some boys had been wading in the creek. I overheard one boy telling how playing hide and seek, he found a hollow spot under the water and a root of the big tree. He said there was an air pocket just big enough to breath.

He said he hid there, and no one could find him." As she continued to talk, Billy remembered having seen the roots of the tree not knowing that she was there.

Betty continued, "The two men were looking for me when I saw them first and I recognized them from before. I knew they were looking for me. "

"Before they saw me, I slipped under the wagon into the water and up under the tree roots. The place under the water was so small, I had to double up. At first, I could not locate the air pocket, I was out of breath when I felt air on my fingers. Then I heard them talking. They knew I had escaped because they could not find my body. I heard them say they would come back after everyone left and pick up my track." Betty Jane stopped for a few moments and then continued. "I was so cold and stiff I stayed for what seemed like hours. When I could not hear them anymore and just could not stand it any longer, I came out. "

When I first saw you, I thought you were one of them when you told me to step behind Arkie and put your shirt and trousers on. I don't know why I did exactly what you told me to do." Then Betty Jane paused with a conscious and dependent look in her eyes she asked a very searching question, "I did the right thing didn't I?"

Betty Jane had been locked into her commitment to Rodney Hartford when she was fourteen years old. She had never dated; she knew next to nothing about how young men acted. She was struggling to understand Billy. What kind of a person was he? How would he treat her? As Billy looked at her, he knew why a man falls in love with a woman. Betty Jane was dependent upon him. He knew he would never let her down. Billy never answered her. She had promised herself to someone else. Billy knew there was something lacking in their relationship, and he was intelligent enough to understand it would never be.

Since they first met, Betty Jane had sought to know what kind of a young man Billy was. She did not know Billy in character or conduct. Everything about him, each situation, each day of their travel, indicated he was a gentleman.

Betty Jane would never get an answer to her question from Billy. Her question went far beyond a mere trust in Billy's comprehension of their relationship. Betty Jane was unaware the question had entered his solitariness. That arena of Billy's thinking was overloaded with a growing love for her. It was increasingly painful for him to love in such a manner, knowing his love would never be reciprocated.

She was treading where angels fear to tread and had no idea what she was doing. She would never get an answer. At this point Billy's relationship of trust and love was infinitely different than Betty Jane's.

Betty would later review their travel and relationship. There was a word best describing it, it was trust. She could trust him. The question she had asked was about trust. She was yet to learn the relationship between trust and love.

Billy and Betty Jane reached the Humboldt River and camped for the evening. They were now conscious of the distance they had come and knew their destination, but they could not contemplate the ending. There had been some 470 miles between them and the town of Sacramento. They were now about 370 miles out.

Billy asked Betty Jane to do something she would not understand until later. It was not the first time he had done this. She knew he had something in mind. Billy looked at her with a pensive expression, "I want you to ride down the path ahead of us and see what makes Lightning break into a gallop."

Betty Jane knew what made most horses gallop, but not Lightning. Nevertheless, she rode down the trail and came back with Lightening galloping without reserve. When she came back, she enthusiastically reported to Billy, "When I heeled his ribs he really took off." Nothing more was said.

The California wagon trail followed the Humboldt River for a good 225 miles before reaching the Humboldt Sink. The riverbank Billy and Betty Jane would travel was a combination of short medium foliage and dry open areas.

Glen Forester's description of the Humboldt River proved accurate. As Billy and Betty Jane neared the Sink, the alkali content would grow progressively worse. Glen had advised Billy they would need to move away from the river when horses and humans required good water and had described in detail those places where Billy would find such water.

The second week after Billy and Betty Jane began to follow the river, they arrived at a small area described by Glen. Betty Jane made fried flour cakes and beans to go with the rabbit Billy had shot earlier. They were about to eat when Billy heard a noise in the bushes next to their camp. Betty Jane froze instantly. Billy quietly walked over to the bushes with his revolver drawn. A middle-aged man and a woman in terrible condition appeared before Billy. The man did not have a gun or anything in hand. The man stammered out, "We're hungry. Do you have any spare food?" Betty Jane was close by Billy's side with a frying pan and flour cakes and immediately offered cakes to both. The couple had not eaten for two days.

They were John and Martha Swanson, trying to get back to Kentucky after a failed venture in California. They were headed towards Fort Hall expecting to join a small group of people returning to Independence, Missouri.

They then told Billy and Betty Jane a sad story. They had been robbed by two men who posed as being hungry and entered their camp. John had described the men; one had shaggy blonde hair that hung down below a filthy brown hat. The other was the voice of the two. He stood six foot two, with a very thin and bony face, and a deep scar down his left cheek. They both wore guns and John Swanson was certain they were killers. The one with the bony face had drawn his gun to shoot both he and Martha when a band of Shoshone Indians appeared on the other side of the

Humboldt River. The evil men ducked for cover; John figured the two men were hated by the friendly Shoshone Braves. John and Martha were left alone in the open. John grabbed Martha's hand and ran until they were totally exhausted. Their horses and everything they owned had been taken, they had escaped with their lives. Since then, they had to follow the river toward Fort Hall at night. They had eaten wild plants and anything they could find. The last two days has been the worst. While John was talking, the starved couple ate the food Betty Jane had prepared. When John finished talking, both he and Martha were embarrassed by eating all the food. Betty

Jane knew their thoughts and was busy making more flour cakes.

The next morning they shared a breakfast of five cutthroat trout Billy had caught from the river. When the two parties parted that morning, Billy gave John Swanson the two Benson horses, one without a saddle and one of the Benson's revolvers. Betty Jane gave them two blankets, a small frying pan, beans, and flour. It was what the Bensons needed most. John and Martha Swanson knew the import of what was given them. They would be forever thankful for the young couple they had met next to the Humboldt River on the way back to Kentucky.

Billy was struck with the realization that not all who travel to California would succeed. For the first time he wondered how he would fare. But Billy had never worried about his future if he had Arkie and his saddle. Billy did not know his future would hold one thing for which he was unprepared. It was something he had never thought or dreamed of about. It would come to him later and it would mean more to him than Arkie and his saddle.

Martha Swanson had observed the relationship between Billy and Betty

Jane. She knew they were not lovers by the emotional space she sensed between them. When she asked Betty Jane about her future, she learned the full story about Rodney Hartford and the wedding in Sacramento. Martha and John had been in Sacramento for a year, and she knew of the Hartford family with a son named Rodney. Had Martha given Betty Jane a report on Rodney Hartford, it would not have been a good one. When John and Martha were on the road after leaving Billy and Betty Jane, Martha remarked, "That girl is about to make the biggest mistake of her life." John countered by saying, "Why didn't you tell her?" Martha said nothing in reply, she knew how impossible that would have been.

Martha's thoughts turned to their son, Randy, who they left behind in Sacramento. Randy had apprenticed with Darcy Whitney, a sawmill owner, and fallen in love with his daughter, Lois. Darcy was impressed with Randy. Martha found comfort in his last words to them before they left Sacramento: "He is a quick learner who had mastered the skills of running a sawmill, and a fine young man. The boy is gifted, and we will look after him." Darcy's daughter, Lois, took note of her father's words – rare words of high praise from him. Darcy would continue to occasionally mention

Randy; how he did this or that, fixed some mechanical malfunction, or suggested ways they could save both time and money in producing the best lumber in town. Lois hung on his every word. Her parents exchanged glances and Mrs. Darcy suggested they invite Randy for dinner. Randy and Lois fell in love, and their engagement was announced two months later.

Martha turned and said to her husband. "I do regret that I did not mention Randy to Billy and Mary Jane."

Early the next morning before Billy and Betty Jane started on their day's journey, Betty Jane had followed Billy a short distance from their campsite, and she had witnessed something extraordinary. Betty Jane knew how to handle a rifle and had shot in contests back east.

A beautiful antelope had passed in front of Billy not more than fifty yards. Billy never raised his rifle. Shortly after, he shot a bounding rabbit at a good seventy-five yards. It was a beautiful head shot few would even have attempted, and it left the rest of the animal edible.

The accuracy and all considered had temporarily invaded Betty Jane's thinking because shortly afterward she asked Billy, "Why did you pass the antelope for the rabbit?" Billy's answer was simple, "We would have wasted a lot of good meat." Betty Jane only wondered about Billy's meaning. Later his meaning struck deeply in Betty Jane's understanding of Billy's character. Everything he did had meaning.

Something about Billy was bothering Betty Jane. She could not understand what it was, so she simply shrugged it off as not important. Truthfully, Billy's presence was in her mind, and she was subconsciously rejecting it. She did not want thoughts of Billy anywhere near her dream with Rodney Hartford. Betty Jane's illusional dream of her life with Rodney Hartford pervaded her thinking. She was unable to allow any contrary thoughts exist. Betty Jane had never been in love; she would have to learn its impact. The daily routine with Billy was revealing a far different person than she had originally thought him to be.

Meanwhile, Billy was very conscious of the emotional gulf between them. He was simply accepted it. He would never be any more than an acquaintance to Betty Jane. Billy knew he was in love with Betty Jane. Betty Jane's unconscious rejection of Billy was painful for Billy. He had managed to accept it in a gentlemanly manner. But he had grown silent and pensive in her presence. Betty Jane knew of his silence, but her state of mind could not comprehend it. She was successfully blocking every attempt concerning Billy. It was her unconscious denial of any serious thoughts regarding Billy that would be so difficult for Betty Jane in future days.

Glen had described in detail the hot, dry, and dangerous area along the river. Billy knew by the terrain they were close to the area Glen had described. It was about forty miles in length and would take more than two days to cross. Glen called it the Sink. Prior to the Sink the water in the river would become undrinkable. Glen had told Billy of the last watering hole set aside from the trail in the treed area in which there was a small lake which was fed by a fresh creek stream. It was the last good water for people and horses for forty miles.

Billy and Betty Jane were about five miles from the sink. The water filled with alkaline was getting worse by the minute. Away from the river Billy noticed a comparatively medium size wooden area. Its size and the color of the trees indicated it might be a good watering area. Billy, Betty Jane, and the horses all needed freshwater. Billy was certain it was the area Glen had mentioned. Sure enough, the wooded area had a creek emptying into a small lake. Billy had dismounted while Betty Jane was still in the saddle on Lightning. Suddenly Arkie nickered, he stared at a clump of bushes, shook his head up and down, tore at the earth with his right hoof, and flared at his nostrils. Billy turned just in time to see two men step out.

Their manner was smooth and silent. Had it not been for Arkie, neither Billy nor Betty Jane would have been aware of their presence. The two men stepped apart which sent an immediate warning to Billy. The tall man to Billy's left had hawk like features and a deep scar on the left side of the face. Billy noticed his gun was in a worn holster and guessed he knew how to use it. The other was shorter and had eyes that were milky blue and stringy blonde hair hanging below a dingy worn brown western hat. Billy had recognized both by the description given by John Swanson. The two men standing before Billy were Jud Barker and Baxter Gordon. They had been Confederate soldiers in the Civil War. They had learned how to kill at Chickamauga. And they never lost the sensation of killing. They took part in raids on helpless victims and had headed west to avoid bounty hunters and detection by authorities.

Jud, realizing they had been detected, spoke first. "We're hungry and wondered if ya had food to spare." Billy thought momentarily, then gave a direct answer, "No we don't, but you got a choice to make." The directness of the answer and the way it was given caught Jud off guard. For a second Jud was unsure of himself, then he flicked his left arm slightly and said in a raspy voice, "How's that?" Without taking his eyes off Jud, Billy answered pointedly "You can hit the trail or go for that gun." Billy knew what Jud would do. When Jud started to pull leather, a slug went right threw his heart.

Billy spun, looking at Baxter; Baxter's gun was slowly leaving his fingers, falling to the ground.

There had been another shot, simultaneous with Billy's. Billy's glance caught Betty Jane's figure slightly slumped over in the saddle, and her gun had a trace of smoke coming from the barrel. She was still in the saddle but trembling badly. Billy lifted her gently from the saddle and tied both Arkie and Lightning to branches. Betty Jane was about to faint when Billy reached her. It was the second time Betty Jane had killed and it was taking a toll on her. Both times she had saved his life, and both times it had been with the Colt .45 Andrew Winstead had given Billy that fateful night in Independence, Missouri.

It was not the same for Billy. Jacob McGovern had told his son he might have to kill to live. Billy understood it had to be done for both Betty Jane and his safety. It was late in the afternoon and Billy wisely decided to remain where they were. He told Betty Jane," We will stay here until morning." Betty Jane nodded and thought "he always seems to do the right thing." Later, Billy would find where Jud and Baxter's horses were staked.

Once again Billy found himself with two extra horses and some extra contents to go through. Betty Jane busied herself with the contents, not finding much of value. Billy did his best in burying the two men. Both Betty Jane and Billy knew these were the men the Swanson's had told them about. However, there was a reluctance in Billy and Betty Jane concerning the killing they had been forced to do. Betty Jane remarked, "I hope this never happens again, where I'm forced to kill someone. I don't believe I could do it." Billy countered, "Betty Jane, you and I could not escape what happened to us. The way we are traveling took us in the path of these men."

After a brief pause, Betty Jane then asked Billy a question, "Why did you act so quickly?" A shadow appeared on Billy's countenance, and he gave this answer; "They had a plan, they knew how and when they would act, when the scar faced man flicked his left arm, it was a signal to the other. I had to gain an edge before they could act. I had to take the one talking first, the other one might get a slug in me, but I would try and take him too." Betty Jane looked hard at Billy,

"But there was me." His answering remark was a simple, "I know." Sometimes Betty Jane was so frustrated by Billy's answers. She had not thought deeply into why he was willing to take a bullet and even die. She thought he just wanted to live and reach California.

Betty Jane later thought about what Billy said, and the way he had said it. She could not seem to understand his full meaning. But she did know the experience, as difficult as it was, had brought about a change in her thinking. She would never be the same again. Her outlook on the value of life was forming. Life was a precious gift given to us by those who love us. Then she thought I am growing up. She was right.

She was down by the creek washing clothes to let dry overnight and preparing for travel in the morning. Her mind had drifted to what was ahead in California. She wanted a home, some children, and a husband to love her. Suddenly, she felt a painful sting in her left ankle. She looked down at a Rattlesnake, coiled and ready to strike again. Betty Jane screamed in panic. Billy came running, saw the snake, and shot it.

He knew from Betty Jane's scream that she knew what had happened. She was looking at the bite mark on her left ankle when Billy picked her up and in a clear commanding voice said, "Don't walk on it.'

Betty Jane was hysterical with fright; she had heard from the wagon folks how serious a rattler bite could be. Betty Jane was already having severe pain, she was dizzy, her eyelids were heavy, and she was getting weaker by the second. Billy put Betty Jane in the sitting position leaning against Arkie's saddle. She was on a small decline with her feet below. Billy went to work immediately. He washed the wound thoroughly and using an ancient Indian remedy his father had told him about. He applied clean plantain leaves which were abundant near the stream and covered the snake bite.

Betty Jane was nauseous and threw up. She was in terrible pain and went in and out of deliriums for three days before beginning to pull out of it. Billy had fed her a brew made up of crushed plantain and a fresh plantain poultice was kept on the wound constantly. It was all Billy could do, and it was enough.

It was a harrowing, agonizing experience for Billy, and he never left her side. Twice he thought he would lose her, each time she rallied. Most of the time she was delirious and talking out of her head. Betty Jane kept mumbling about Rodney and how handsome he was. Billy could only surmise it was her fiancé in California she was referring to. On the fifth day after the snakebite Billy thought they could travel again. Mary Jane was still weak but able to travel.

Billy was about to start loading the horses. Betty Jane whispered to him, "Look on the other side of the lake." There were six Shoshone Indian braves. The first thing Billy noted about them was two of them on one horse.

Glen had told Billy much about the Shoshone, they were a peaceful people and usually they wanted to trade. Glen had even given Billy some basic signs to communicate with them. Billy was quite sure he knew what they wanted.

After looking them over carefully, Billy then gave the peace sign and the lead Shoshone brave responded with a like sign. Their exchange of peace signs was tantamount to a welcome by both parties. The Shoshone Braves then rode around the small lake for a parley.

Billy told Betty Jane to move back out of view. Billy knew they had already seen her, but it was his way of telling them he did not want her bothered. They knew what he had done and why. Billy welcomed the braves into camp and had them seated.

Presently they were able to communicate; they wanted to trade. Billy then asked them what they wanted. They wanted to trade for a horse. He asked them what they had to trade. Betty Jane was listening for two painful hours wondering what Billy was doing. Each time the braves offered Billy something he looked it over then shook his head no.

Finally, Billy started to get up, but the Braves quickly asked him to be seated. They wanted to know what he wanted. Billy had known from the beginning what he wanted.

Two of the Indians had large sheepskin water bags on their horses. Billy held two fingers up and pointed to the water bags. There was an immediate state of alarm between the Shoshone braves, followed by a loud conversation. Soon the leader of the braves held up one finger, pointing to a water bag. Billy shook his head and again started to get up, but again the leader motioned for Billy to stay seated. Again, there was a loud animated discussion among the braves. Finally, their leader turned to Billy holding up two fingers and it was a done deal. The Braves gave Billy the two sheepskin water bags after which Billy brought out the two horses they had acquired from the thieves. After some time of a quarrel among the natives, they chose the larger horse.

The Shoshone Braves had noticed two graves, and it was not the first time they had seen the two horses. They knew who they had belonged to and felt indebted to Red Shirt. They had already heard of Red Shirt. Billy did not know it, but he had gained a reputation of respect among several of the tribes. Billy would take care of their people if needed, and Red Shirt was considered a great warrior and a friend among all the Native Americans who had dealt with him.

Red Shirt and his young lady were not to be harmed. Red Shirt had taken out two men the Shoshone Braves hated. They would talk of this at their campfire.

The Shoshone leader spoke of Red Shirt in their conversation. Billy asked, "Who is Red Shirt? "The Shoshone chief turned to his Braves and told him what Billy had asked. There was a huge laughter by all the braves. Betty Jane, who had been watching the proceedings with care and concern, noted one of the heavier seated warriors laughed so hard he almost tipped over. The Shoshone leader turned to Billy and pointed right at Billy's chest. "You Red Shirt." The braves laughed again, and Billy laughed with them. Betty Jane later asked Billy why they had laughed. He told her, and Betty Jane laughed also.

Shortly after, Billy and Betty Jane were on the trail again. Billy had both sheepskins full of fresh water loaded on the third horse. Billy, Betty Jane, and the horses would know the import of the sheepskins of water as they traveled across the forty-mile Sink area. Glen had told Billy he would be August when he reached the Sink. It would be best if they traveled at night as it would be cooler. Glen said it took the wagon train three days to cross the Sink. Billy and Betty Jane made it in two and a half days.

It was midafternoon. Billy and Betty Jane were angling toward the southwestern tip of the Sierra Nevada Mountain range when they both noticed the darkening skies over the mountain range. Billy had heard of those immediate flash floods and had noticed at a distance the arroyo with steep banks directly in front of them. They had to pass directly through the arroyo to follow their designated trail to reach Sacramento. Billy reigned up, cutting the reign to the pack horse. Betty Jane pulled even looking at Billy for some explanation. Without taking his eyes off the clouds Billy simply stated, "We need to hurry past the dip up yonder." With that he gave Arkie the command, but Betty Jane and Lightning were already moving at a clip. Meanwhile, Arkie did not like Lightning moving out ahead so he started to pull even with Lightning, but Lightning just pulled out further. They had entered the arroyo when Billy heard and saw a six-foot wave of water sweeping down at them and they were directly in its path. Billy healed Arkie and they were flat out moving, but Lightning and Betty Jane were already climbing out the other side of the arroyo. Billy and Arkie pulled out following with water hitting the back of Arkie's legs. And last and fortunately, to Billy's amazement the pack horse had followed and made it also.

The sight of water crashing by made Betty Jane tremble as she remembered Billy having her discover what made Lightning move out fast. She had done just that. Lightning and Arkie both know what was needed of them. Billy and Betty Jane were safe on the Sacramento side of the arroyo.

They escaped a dangerous situation again because of some prior thinking and action of Billy. It was getting to be a pattern of behavior for Betty Jane. From the very beginning of their meeting, she had done what Billy asked. She did not understand why she had done it, but each action had been crucial to their survival. Subconsciously Betty Jane was changing her initial estimate of Billy McGovern.

On Billy's part, he later would be struck with the swiftness of Betty Janes reaction. Neither Billy nor Betty Jane had yet realized how dependent she was on his every move. The realization began to dawn in Billy's consciousness how sharply attuned to every situation Betty Jane had been. Twice she had saved his life and she had known immediately what to do in the face of the flash flooded arroyo.

Billy's attachment to Betty Jane was growing every day on the trail to Sacramento. Her unconscious dependence upon him from the very beginning of their relationship made Billy feel something he had never experienced before; Billy felt responsible for Betty Jane, and despite her closed mind regarding anyone other than Rodney Hartford, Billy and Betty Jane's relationship made him feel like a man. But the growing attachment co-existed with a hopeless sense of pain; the attachment would never have real meaning. Billy wisely concluded as soon as they reached Sacramento, he would remove himself from Betty Jane's presence.

After escaping the dangerous flash flood, and traveling further southwest, Billy found the Truckee River without too much difficulty. They replenished at Truckee Lake and headed for their last major challenge before reaching their destination. Before they started to climb up the east side of the pass Billy remark to Betty Jane, "We're about ninety miles out." Betty Jane asked, "How many days?" Billy answered, "I believe five to six days. I am told it's a rough climb on our side but a gradual decent on the

West side, and the evenings are very cold on the pass."

That evening by the campfire Betty Jane had long wanted to ask Billy about his first look at her back on the trail. She mentioned the time and the place and then asked, "Why did you look at me that way?" Billy looked at her with a penetrating glance, "Betty Jane, you don't have the right to know the answer to that question, and besides, if I told you, it wouldn't help either of us." His answer was about the last words he would speak to her on the remaining journey.

Those words were like a slap of cold water thrown on her face. At first, she thought he was rude and unkind with his answer. Then she realized he hadnot said it rudely or in an unkind manner. He had said it as a matter of fact.

The ascent to the top of Donner's Pass was rugged, dangerous, and risky. Arkie navigated it well but did not like it. Lightning just took it like it was an everyday experience. In the evening of the second day from Truckee Lake, they were camped somewhere near the summit of the pass. Billy had killed a rabbit and they had eaten well and retired for the evening. Billy had built a fire, but it was downright cold. Betty Jane had the Buffalo hide and Billy had two blankets.

It was sometime near midnight when Billy was awakened by a movement against his back. It was Betty Jane. She was shivering so bad her teeth were making a noise. She said simply, "I'm cold" as she snuggled up to his back. Billy took the buffalo hide tucked it behind Betty Jane and wrapped the rest around his body. The two blankets he threw over the top of them from a sitting position. He then positioned himself closely to Betty Jane. Betty Jane helped by moving as close as she could against Billy's back.

Shortly after the heat of their body stopped Betty Janes trembling. A few moments later Billy sensed Betty Jane's breathing normalized. She was asleep.

Billy could not understand Betty Jane. She treated him as if he had no feelings. He was a man with normal passions. He knew he loved her, but he was slowly losing respect for her. She was annihilating something she would regret ever having done. Betty Jane did not understand the relation of trust and love in a true relationship. The next morning and the rest of the trip nothing was said of what had taken place that evening.

PART III

SACRAMENTO

Billy and Arkie were a length ahead of Betty Jane and Lightning. They were just coming slowly over a small rise, when Betty Jane let out a little scream, "There's Sacramento." Billy answered her, "I believe you're right."

There was an indescribable feeling of relief by both as they drew nearer to the destination they had struggled to reach. Betty Jane had only dreamed of it; with Billy it was different. Sacramento was a place of challenge.

Betty Jane had noticed Billy to be unusually silent the last few days. He had told her in all probability they would reach Sacramento sometime today. He never said too much anyway, so Betty Jane did not bother to ask him anything about his silence.

With a stroke of luck, they located the small, neat home of Betty Jane's Aunt, Erma Riggs. As they rode up to the residence, Billy immediately saw Betty Jane would have no place for Lightning. Without any explanation, he spoke, "I can take Lightning with me."

She had not thought about it but now the whole situation was before her. She started to cry when she got down from Lightning. She stepped near Lightning's head and hugged him. Lightning knew what was going on, he had grown accustomed to Betty Jane. When Lightning nickered and nudged with his nose, Betty Jane cried some more.

After Billy met Mrs. Riggs, he very awkwardly said goodbye to Betty Jane and left immediately. Erma Riggs pondered why such a pleasant young man wanted to leave so quickly. Aunt Erma watched Betty Jane as Billy and the horses rode off in the direction, she had given him to the Richards ranch. Erma Riggs wondered if Betty Jane was watching Billy or Lightning.

Billy would have said she is watching Lightning. Betty Jane had hugged Lightning, and hardly said a word to Billy. It hurt badly, Billy did not want to admit it, but it did.

There was something else of enormous impact to both young people that neither of them totally comprehended at this juncture. It had vaguely crossed Billy's mind, but he had refused to pursue the thought. Its painful presence would frequently cross his mind in future days. The absence of Betty Jane's presence would cast a shadow and bring a sullen mood to Billy. The shadow would diminish some in future days largely because of a young lady Billy was yet to meet-Evelyn Richards, Billy's cousin. Evelyn would understand and help Billy through it.

Betty Jane, on the other hand, was unaware of the impact of being with Billy and the togetherness in all they had been forced to face.

On the morning of the next day Betty Jane spoke to her aunt. "Aunt Erma, I am not overly anxious to relate all that happened on our trip here. But I have this to say. Billy McGovern was a perfect gentleman in every respect." Aunt Erma's thinking relaxed, for she had wondered what kind of a relationship the two young people had. Aunt Erma had sensed the emotional gap between her niece and Billy. Betty Jane wanted to continue, but something interrupted her thinking, and she uttered to herself. "Oh, why is he always there."

Aunt Erma heard and took note of the way her niece said it. Betty Jane proceeded to inform her aunt of the entire events of the trip. Betty Jane had to shake her thinking and she told her Aunt Erma of all that had happened. It was like she was in Billy's presence, and she was saying things he would say. Sometimes she looked up from what she was saying, thinking he was there. It was so unconscious it irritated her. Why was Billy always in her thinking? After explaining her irritation to her Aunt Erma, Betty Jane confessed, "I don't understand it, why is Billy McGovern always on my mind." Erma Riggs was beginning to get the picture.

Erma Riggs knew of Rodney Hartford just as Martha Swanson and she had an identical understanding of his character Martha had. Betty Jane would be making the biggest mistake of her life in pursuing Rodney Hartford.

Billy headed out looking for the livery stable and very soon found what he was looking for. An elderly gentleman by the name of Pete was in charge. After Pete tended and grained the two horses. Billy inquired of Pete, "Would you know of William Richards?" Ole Pete laughed and remark, "Why everyone in Sacramento knows Will Richards. What you want with him?"

Before Billy could continue, Ole Pete remarked again, "That's two mighty fine-looking horses you're a toting. They look a mite tired though. Say young man, you look like you been a traveling a distance, where ya from?" Billy laughed and said, "Tennessee." Ole Pete laughed and said,

"Yeah, I bet you are." Billy paid Ole Pete, mounted Arkie, and with Lightning in tow set out for Will Richard's spread.

An hour later Billy arrived at the biggest ranch house and buildings he had ever seen. As he neared the ranch house, a young ranch hand came forward to meet Billy. The ranch hand remarked, "Looks like you have been on the trail a while." Taking the reins from Billy he asked, "You want these horses grained? By the way, I think you're the one they were hoping would show up." Billy liked the young man immediately and Billy found out later he had reason to like him.

Walking up on a huge porch which went all the way around the house, Billy knocked on the door. An attractive young lady answered the door, "May I help you?" She asked. Billy looked at her and said, "I'd like to see Will Richards." She answered, "Whom should I say wants to see him?" Billy said, "Tell him it's Billy McGovern." Evelyn Richards stepped back and yelled, "Dad and Mom come quick, you won't believe who is here!"

An hour later at the dinner table every eye was on Billy as questions were being fired at him from every angle. Will

Richard was so proud of his namesake. He told Billy, "My sister Mary named you after me." At their insistence, the evening was spent telling his uncle, aunt, and his cousin everything. Well, not everything, he left out any mention of Betty Jane.

Evelyn got the full report two days later from Mrs. Riggs. Erma Riggs wisely cautioned Evelyn, "Betty Jane may be a real tender spot for Billy, you will do well to go softly." Two things Evelyn and Mrs. Riggs agreed upon: Evelyn should go carefully with Billy, and Betty Jane was making a costly mistake with her interest in Rodney Hartford.

Evelyn Richards was by nature a truly kind and helpful person. It was not long before she realized Billy McGovern was an unusually talented young man, but he would need some help in acclimating himself to the young life in California.

Evelyn had a genuine concern for her cousin's success in meeting other young people in Sacramento society. She wanted to introduce him to a fine class of young ladies. Her cousin would need a wife. Evelyn was known and respected by all who knew her, and she had a plan for Billy. She would teach him the California style of dancing, table manners, speaking skills, and polite etiquette in every respect.

The third day after Betty Jane and Billy arrived in Sacramento the Hartford's came to meet Betty Jane at the Riggs household. Rodney greeted Betty Jane with a kiss that she did not like. That was not all, she noticed how little muscle he had, and he was flabby.

It was true he was indeed handsome, but his mannerisms bordered on being downright rude. While in Rodney's presence, Betty Jane's mind drifted to another young man with whom had spent five months. Betty Jane then shook the thought off. She said to herself "I must not think that way." But before shifting thought she caught her Aunt

Erma's eye. It was as though Aunt Erma read her mind. Aunt Erma knew exactly what Betty Jane was thinking.

At the Hartford's invite, Rodney and Betty Jane would spend some time together on the following evening at the Hartford residence. When they parted that evening Rodney lingered on the porch with Betty Jane his manners were so rude, she had to dismiss yourself. She did not like it when he touched her. His touch was demanding and fresh like to Betty Jane.

After Rodney departed her aunt was waiting and said very calmly, "You don't have to go through with it if you think better." Betty Jane did not know what to say. She sought for an answer but there was none. She said nothing and went to her bedroom, but she was beginning to have some second thoughts on her own.

She wanted to give Rodney every chance before she made any decision regarding their future. However, she was receiving some tell-tale hints from people she did not even know. She told Aunt Erma the following morning about two young ladies who gave her indignant stares while shopping. Betty Jane asked "Why did they do that? They looked at me like I had done something wrong."

With Betty Jane's question, Aunt Erma decided it was time someone give Betty Jane the full story concerning Rodney Hartford before it was too late. Aunt Erma told the full story of Rodney's cloudy behavior with unsuspecting young ladies. She told Betty Jane about the young lady whose pregnancy was so humiliating to the girl's family they had to leave the area.

All what Aunt Erma told her brought a sadness to Betty Jane. She had anticipated, she had planned, and she had sacrificed for a happy marriage with Rodney Hartford since she was fourteen years old.

Betty Jane reviewed all she had been through to reach California. She had thought and dreamed of how Rodney had the same dedication and commitment to their future together. Betty Jane knew the dream was over.

The knowledge imparted to her by Aunt Erma, the sentiment of expression indicated by the two young ladies, and others she had never expressed to her Aunt Erma, was changing her mind about her future. Most of all it was her perception of the feelings she experienced when with Rodney. The revolting feelings she had when he touched her gave her a negative feeling of their relationship. Betty Jane told Aunt

Erma, "There is something about him I don't like.

She would have Aunt Erma inform the Hartford family she was sick and would not be able to attend the meeting planned. Rodney had boasted to his friends he was going to marry the most beautiful girl in Sacramento, it was a blow to his ego when Betty Jane wanted nothing to do with him. He had tried to see her on several occasions, each time she was unavailable.

It was not long before the fascinating and complete story of Billy and Betty Jane's dangerous journey from Fort Hall to Sacramento was known and favored by all the young people in the Sacramento area.

It was three weeks later when at a dance for young people Rodney saw Betty Jane. By now he had heard all about how she had been rescued by Billy McGovern and brought safely to Sacramento. He had been waiting for a chance to show off when he met Billy McGovern.

He was told that the tall young man dancing with Evelyn Richard was indeed Billy McGovern. He would have a chance to get even with Betty Jane and make Billy look bad before the other young people. Rodney had spent some time training how to hit with his fist and he would try it out on Billy.

Rodney Hartford marched right up in front of Billy and Evelyn and spoke in a loud voice so everyone could hear. "So you are the great Billy McGovern who compromised Betty Jane while rescuing her. You must be really proud of yourself." While saying this Rodney, threw a punch at Billy. Billy moved Evelyn out of the way, as Rodney's punched grazed Billy's left cheek. Billy did not mind what Rodney said about him, but when he implicated Betty Jane, Billy was stark mad.

Rodney was getting ready to throw another punch when Billy hit him with a straight left jab to the nose. Billy felt cartilage bone give with his blow. Billy was not finished. He hit Rodney with a right uppercut to the jaw, and again Billy felt the bone give. Rodney stumbled backwards and fell on the seat of his pants. Billy walked right up in front of Rodney and said so everyone could hear, especially Betty Jane, who had heard what Rodney Hartford had said about her. "Mister, I do not know who you are, but you told a lie about Betty Jane. Nothing of the sort ever happened. She was a lady in every respect. Why would you say such a thing?"

The musicians came to the rescue and promptly started another number. The dancing continued. Two of Rodney's friends carried him out. Rodney's nose was flattened out against his face and his jaw alignment was altered so he was not so handsome.

The results of Rodney's ill-mannered tirade had an opposite effect upon the young people who witnessed the event. They gained admiration for both Betty Jane and Billy. Billy's defense of Betty Jane's integrity had a distinct ring of truth. Both were admired, and one young person said their relationship was, "The way things ought to be."

That evening Betty Jane shared the happenings at the dance with Aunt Erma. Aunt Erma spoke well of Billy's defense of Betty Jane's character. She then added, "Billy saved your reputation by his words and actions." Betty Jane thought a moment and then commented, "I don't understand why it bothers me when he dances with the other young ladies. I saw him dancing with Evelyn Richards tonight and for some reason I did not like it. I should be happy for him." Aunt Erma knew Betty Jane had never been in love before. Betty Jane was starting to awaken to a very painful reality. She was in love with Billy McGovern, and she was starting to realize it.

The following week Betty Jane was increasingly unhappy. Her Aunt watched her carefully, knowing it was only a question of time before Betty Jane would need to confide in her.

One evening a week later, Betty Jane asked to speak with her aunt. Aunt Erma noticed Mary Jane's eyes were swollen, she had been crying. Betty Jane started out by saying "The morning after Billy rescued me from the horrible wagon train incident, I had cleaned up, and Billy looked at me for the first time. I could not understand his look. The depth of his look frightened me. Now I understand his look, it was a look of "Forever." Aunt Erma, as I recollect everything that took place with Billy, he must have cared for me from the very beginning. He gave me his extra shirt and trousers, he put the buffalo robe around me, he lifted me up like a feather and put me on Arkie. He fought those evil men and when I had the snake bite, he was at my side day and night."

"Aunt Erma, there is something else that happened." She then told Aunt Erma about the freezing night near the top of

Donner's Pass. She trusted him so explicitly she could snuggle up to him knowing he would protect her and respect her. "Aunt Erma, it was a dangerous and stupid thing to do. What must he think of me? I have been blind, Aunt Erma. I have made the biggest mistake of my life. I took all that for granted. When he rode away after bringing me here, I never even thanked him."

With that, Betty Jane burst into tears. "Aunt Erma, I must have killed any feeling he could have ever had for me. When we were at the dance, he never even looked my way. Aunt Erma, I know

Billy McGovern. Billy is not taken in by fancy looks and nice dress, he cares for character. I have shown him absolutely nothing."

Betty Jane continued, "All the time I was thinking about Rodney Hartford, I was walking by a person who was so much more than I ever dreamed could even exist. I cannot take Billy out of my mind, I wonder where he is, who is he talking to at this moment, does he ever think of me?" Betty Jane burst into tears again. Aunt Erma took Betty Jane in her arms and comforted her.

Then Aunt Erma spoke right to the point. "Betty Jane, I believe the first thing you must do is know your mind. Billy McGovern may never change his mind and care for you again, but if he does it will not be for someone who is half-hearted. You must make up your mind."

"There is an Old West saying about a young lady who picks out her man, 'She sets her bonnet.' And then she bakes him a pie, she makes him a shirt and her actions show her heart. You must do the same Betty Jane. You must show Billy McGovern he is the only man you will ever be happy with. If you do not feel that way, you need to forget it."

The following week Betty Jane thought it through, and she knew her mind. She went to her aunt, "Aunt Erma, I have a plan. Do you have a sewing machine?" "Of course, I do." was her aunt's reply.

That afternoon Betty Jane went shopping and for the next week she spent all her time in her room. Aunt Erma could hear the sewing machine almost nonstop. It was a new peddle lock stitch machine Betty Jane had learned on back East in Boston. Aunt Erma had been fortunate in picking it up from a family heading back East. They were cutting down on their travel load, Aunt Erma was happy to assist them.

Betty Jane was an excellent seamstress. She could make anything and everything she made was beautiful. She had no trouble determining Billy's size, she remembered so well putting her arms around Billy on their first ride on Arkie. There were also the subsequent days of constantly being in his presence.

While working on her project and reviewing Billy's actual size her mind returned to their time together. Her thoughts brought back things she had never given any thought to at the time. It was the way Billy thought and the way he carried himself. Betty Jane realized she was always protected whatever took place. Her meditating brought her to conclude two facts; Billy McGovern was special in so many respects, and secondly, Billy meant so much to her, if she lost him, there would be a void in her life forever. What she was doing now was a labor of love. She would do her best, and she did just that.

When she finally finished, she took the item she had made and wrapped it neatly with a little blue bow. She penned a short note in beautiful hand script and attached the little sealed card to the package.

Two days later the package arrived at the Richard's residence. Evelyn and her mother, Molly Richard, were quite excited to find out who would send Billy a package and especially one so beautifully wrapped. Billy had no idea who it was from, and he very carefully read the little note attached.

Billy did not read it aloud, but when finished reading it his countenance had changed, but he continued to open the package. He removed the contents and held it up to his shoulders. It was a red shirt, the stitching and everything about it was so beautifully done, the two ladies' breath was taken.

Billy turned the shirt around to look at the pockets, then he saw the beautiful, embroidered words across the top of the left pocket, "Red Shirt." Billy looked at it and was stunned. He never said a word, he just left the room.

Billy took the shirt with him, but the little card had dropped to the floor. Evelyn retrieved it and could not help reading it to her mother. It was handwritten in beautiful script. "To Billy McGovern" and below it read, "To someone who has done so very much for me, and I never even thanked him." It was signed, "Betty Jane Watson." After hearing it read, Molly said to her daughter, "I think she's set her bonnet." Molly Richard thought a moment more, and commented, "Did you see the stitch work on that shirt, I don't ever recall seeing more beautiful work, that young girl must be something very special." Evelyn thought carefully, then commented, "I just hope she knows what she's doing."

Three evenings later the monthly young people's dance was held and since it was within walking distance from the Riggs home, Betty Jane was there. Billy was there also. He was dancing with a young lady Evelyn had introduced him to when he saw Betty Jane. She was dancing with a nice-looking young man who had simply walked up and asked her if she would like to dance. She was sitting idle and did not see how she could refuse. Billy felt something like a deep hurt inside when he saw her dancing with the young man. As soon as the music stopped, he was standing in front of her, "May I have this next dance?" "It would be my pleasure," Betty Jane replied.

Neither Billy nor Betty Jane knew what the next number would be. It was a waltz. Evelyn had spent some time with Billy and waltzes, and he had become quite efficient and smooth at it. And in no time at all Betty Jane and Billy were gliding across the floor, they were so taken up looking at each other and the dance, they did not see the floor had emptied for them.

Their dance was so beautiful, the other young people had cleared the floor. When the dance ended, they received a huge ovation. Since the dance was over, Billy did not waste any time. He asked Betty Jane if he could see her home. Betty Jane's heart was strangely warmed when he asked her. They exchanged some small talk as they rode together, and at the door he cleared his throat, "Betty Jane, would you mind if I called on you?"

Mary Jane was as cool as could be, "Billy why don't you come over this Friday evening for a meal, say at six." As Billy rode home on the buckboard, he was strangely happy. The cloud that had hung over Billy ever since he did not know when, was beginning to lift. He wanted Friday evening to be right now, he did not want to wait.

Evelyn Richards was very protective of Billy's well-being. She understood something about the cloud of unhappy discontent that Billy had lived under since showing up at the ranch. It was not easy for Evelyn to read Billy at first, but she finally determined it had something to do with the young lady he had brought with him from the destroyed wagon train.

Evelyn could not understand how the young lady, Betty Jane Watson, could be with Billy all these months of travel, and not read the profound difference between Rodney Hartford and Billy McGovern. Evelyn did not want to destroy Billy's happiness and she did not want anyone else to do it either.

The next day after the dance, Evelyn Richards met Betty Jane while shopping in Sacramento. Both young ladies knew of each other from a distance but had never conversed., After greeting and exchanging names, Betty Jane could see that Evelyn wanted to say something to her, so Betty Jane suggested they find a comfortable sitting area where they might have some tea and visit. Both young ladies knew something of each other. Betty Jane knew that Evelyn was Billy's cousin and had spent time with Billy acclimating him with the Sacramento life. Evelyn, on the other hand, was very much aware of her own endeavor to shift Billy's affection from a hopeless situation with a young lady already promised, and Betty Jane was the young lady.

Evelyn began by complimenting Betty Jane on the beauty of the waltz performed by Betty Jane and Billy at the most recent dance. Evelyn continued, "Billy informed me that you had never danced together before, but I thought since you had spent so much time together coming from that dreadful experience on the wagon train, that you may have been quite familiar with everything about Billy."

Evelyn paused for a moment and then continued, "I have a question I'd like you to answer for me. Your association with Billy for months on the wagon train and your betrothal to marry someone like

Rodney Hartford and Billy's own words to me about your complete shutting Billy out of your thinking, how could you do such a thing? In fact, Billy said when he left you at Mrs. Riggs home, you hugged Lightning the horse and barely said goodbye to Billy. Do you have any idea what this was doing to a young man who was deeply in love with you?"

"From the time you and Billy arrived, I have earnestly spent a great deal of time trying to help him put his life back together." Evelyn stopped and spoke directly to Betty Jane. "Betty Jane, Billy's affections are not a plaything you can pick up and lay down whenever you want. The difference between Billy McGovern and Rodney Hartford is so far apart. Betty Jane, what are your intentions with Billy, why are you now showing an interest in him?"

It was Betty Jane's turn. She knew whatever she said would be critical to her future with Billy. Evelyn had been right in every respect. Betty Jane didn't waste any time, "I know that in many cases where a person approaches another the way you have approached me, the answer might be simple, "it's none of your business." I do not know you or your relationship with Billy, but I know you are concern for Billy is genuine. Because of that I want to relate the full story to you."

Betty Jane then went into her early beginnings with Rodney Hartford, of her dream for a happy marriage with Rodney, of her sacrifice for her dream, of all her prayers and hopes and further of her travel across the continent. She never knew Rodney Hartford nor was ever in love with him. She was in love with the future.

Betty Jane continued with her rescue from the massacre grounds by Billy, and how she had treated Billy so ill and how she had taken everything he had done for her for granted. Betty Jane told Evelyn of her telling her Aunt Erma how Billy was always in her thinking. She could not understand why she kept thinking he was standing next to her when he was not even there. Betty Jane even told Evelyn about the Red Shirt.

Then she related the evening at Aunt Erma's when she first met Rodney Hartford, how when he touched her the terrible feelings she experienced. There was something about Rodney's presence that turned Betty Jane off completely.

Aunt Erma decided it was high time Betty Jane should know the full story about Rodney Hartford. After hearing it, she broke up with Rodney immediately. Rodney was so upset he decided to ruin Betty Jane and Billy's characters at the dance.

Betty Jane started to cry when she told Evelyn every item of how she had treated Billy so ill and how she had taken everything he had done for her for granted. At this point Betty Jane started to sob. Betty Jane's sorrow was so intense It was gut wrenching for Evelyn to hear the anguish in it. She slid over and took Betty Jane in her arms.

Evelyn realized for the first time, something she had not expected. The emotional distance between Betty Jane and Billy was equal on both sides. Their love for each other was painfully divided and had to be brought together. Evelyn realized she had the answer to the question she had asked Betty Jane and Evelyn knew she would do everything she could to bring Betty Jane and Billy together.

Two evenings later when Billy was getting ready to leave for the Riggs home, Evelyn remark to Billy, "Why don't you wear your red shirt tonight." Billy turned and said, "You know, that's a good idea. I think I will." Billy changed shirts. Molly Richards later spoke too

Evelyn, "What are you so happy about tonight." Evelyn just smiled.

That evening was the most memorable time for Betty Jane and Billy. The meal was excellent, and Billy commented on it several times. When Billy was served a large slice of fresh baked apple pie he remarked, Mrs. Riggs, "You make an apple pie, I've never tasted before." Mrs. Riggs said, "Land's sake I didn't cook anything, Betty Jane did it all." Billy turned to Betty Jane, "I should have known, so many times on the trail you made so much when we had so little."

Mrs. Riggs commented what a beautiful shirt Billy was wearing. Billy knew exactly what he was doing when he answered, "Yes, it was made by a very special person." When he said it, Betty Jane immediately left the room.

Erma Riggs asked Billy, "Did Betty Jane make it?" "She most certainly did" was Billy's answer. Betty returned to the room shortly after, and with some coaching, Billy told them all about Jacob and Mary McGovern and his home as a boy. Betty Jane listened intently knowing how important it would be.

The following afternoon at the Richards Ranch, Evelyn asked Billy to join her in the family library. Evelyn knew Betty Jane would never be able to make it through telling Billy all she had told her. Evelyn told Billy everything, it gave Billy an understanding of the relationship he and Betty Jane had on the trail from Fort Hall to Sacramento.

Evelyn's report made Billy happy. Billy knew he was very much in love with Betty Jane, and he would never be happy without Betty Jane's love. He knew from what Evelyn had told him that Betty Jane either loved him or thought much of him. Billy did not waste any time. Shortly after, he was at the Riggs House. Aunt Erma saw him ride up, grabbed her purse and shopping bag, and headed out the door. She gave Billy a short wave as she turned toward town. She did not need to be told why Billy was there.

Betty Jane answered the door and Billy stood before her with the same look in his eyes he had that first day saw her. Only this time she knew what the look meant. Betty Jane started to tremble and cry but she was in Billy arms so quickly,

Billy spoke clearly, "Betty Jane, I don't ever want to be apart from you. I loved you the first moment I saw you. When you stepped out of the water covered with mud, I looked into your eyes and the strangest sensation hit me. I loved you that very moment."

Billy thought of all the times on their trip when he had felt an emotional distance between them, it seemed insurmountable. At that moment Billy just wanted to hold Betty Jane in his arms. Betty Jane on the other hand, thought of how blind and foolish she had been.

That evening they did something that would be repeated in the following years. Billy and Betty Jane looked into each other's eyes, and he saw the "forever" look in her eyes. Billy spoke out while looking into Betty Jane's eyes, "When I was in Dyersburg, I had a strong, almost insurmountable feeling that my destiny was in California. Betty Jane, you are a part of that destiny. I cannot bear the thought that I might never have met you."

Betty Jane put her fingers on Billy's lips and momentary stopped him from speaking. She wanted to say something. "Billy, the morning after you rescued me and you looked at me for the first time, and later when I so thoughtlessly tried to have you explain why you looked at me in that manner, I know now, and I believe from my first words that I ever spoke to you, I knew then. It was a "forever" look in your eyes. Billy, when I was in Boston I felt so strongly, I thought I would be with Rodney, but the minute I was with him it was so terrible, I knew I could never love him and that I never had loved him."

"When we arrived here, I could not understand why I kept thinking of you. I told Aunt Erma I could not understand why you kept coming to my mind. Then I started to review all the things that happened on our trip here. Billy, you are the person I dreamed of being with. I was so foolish, I never even realized it. How can you ever forgive me?" Billy put his finger on Betty Jane's lips, stopping her from saying a word, and did something he felt compelled to do. Taking her hand, he knelt. "Betty Jane, will you marry me?" Betty Jane looked into Billy's eyes and said "yes."

Later that evening Betty Jane asked Billy what changed his mind. Billy told her about Evelyn's report to him. Then he smiled and said, "The shirt and the pie helped." And in truth they had.

When Billy returned to the Richard's ranch, Evelyn was waiting for him. "Well, what happened?" Billy smiled and said, "She asked me to marry her." Evelyn slugged Billy a good one and laughed.

While Billy and Betty Jane were planning their wedding, the new Transcontinental Railroad brought an important check from the Swearengen family in Tennessee. It was the balance of what was owed for the property purchased from Billy in Dyersburg.

Raymond Swearengen, the oldest Swearengen son, had moved on to the McGovern spread and had an excellent year. Between the two farms and some borrowed money, they paid the total owed to Billy. It was a good move for the

Swearengens and very timely for Billy and Betty Jane.

Hubert and Dorothy Williams had just posted a sizable piece of property five miles East of Sacramento. They were anxious to sell and wanted to move back to the East Coast. Dorothy's mother was near the end and Dorothy was adamant about returning to the East to see her mother. A local banker had offered a ridiculously low amount of money for the property, knowing the Williams needed an immediate sale. The banker thought to take advantage of the situation. When the banker did not receive an immediate go ahead from the Williams, he gave up his interest in the property. They were left without a buyer who had the financial resources to make the purchase.

Billy and Betty Jane had looked at the property, and Betty Jane had fallen in love with the way it was situated. At the entrance of the property there was a slight raise in the land overlooking a small lake which was fed by a mountain stream. Immediately past the lake was a vast meadow. The property was surrounded by a variety of different trees. There were California Oak, Valley Oak, Blue Oak, Live Oak, and the interior was lined with Grey Pine, all of which made a beautiful surrounding. It was not a small property. Both Billy and Betty Jane were excited about its prospects.

Dorothy Williams had taken a liking to Betty Jane and really wanted Billy and Betty Jane to have the property. Dorothy shared her dream of the placement of the ranch home, the bunkhouse, and the vineyard she wanted to plant. All of which was very much the same as Billy and Betty Jane had envisioned after seeing the property.

Hubert and Dorothy offered it to them for an incredibly fair price, but Billy and Betty Jane at the time did not have their money from Dyersburg and were unable to make an offer.

Meanwhile the Williams family was growing hopeful that something would break when they discovered through William Richards that Billy and Betty Jane had just received a sizable amount of cash. They immediately reached Billy through William Richards and an attractive offer was made which made both Billy and Betty Jane happy. Shortly after the transaction was completed Billy had money left over and wasted no time in starting a building program.

Billy needed an individual who could operate the sawmill that came with the property and sought his uncle's advice. Will Richards said "Billy, there is a particularly good young apprentice working at Darcy Whitney's sawmill. Let me talk it over with Darcy."

A week later, Will and Billy rode to the sawmill. Darcy made the formal introductions "Randy, this is my friend Will Richards, and his nephew, Billy McGovern." Randy Swanson was so overwhelmed, he embraced Billy, and through tear-stained eyes, he said "You are the one who met my father and mother on the way back to Kentucky, aren't you? You and a young lady rescued them from starving and gave them horses, supplies, and everything they needed to make it to Fort Hall." Martha's long letter to Randy and Lois had described the Swanson's journey and safe arrival back to Kentucky in detail, including Billy and Betty Jane's great act of kindness.

Randy was so eager to assist Billy, he wanted to donate his work. Billy would not have it. Randy and his wife Lois became instant friends with Billy and Betty Jane. Later, Billy would tell Randy of their meeting with Jud Barker and Baxter Gordon. Lois was eager to relay all of this to John and Martha Swanson, in Kentucky. As Martha read the letter to her husband, she paused several times to catch her breath, and parse the contents. She summed up the letter, "This is all good news. Randy and Lois are doing well, the men who robbed us met their fate, and Betty Jane did not make the mistake of marrying Rodney. John, there's a beautiful story behind that last one." And to that, John smiled, and nodded his agreement.

Billy had already picked out a logging crew and foreman among the ranch hands, and in short order, Randolph Swanson had Billy's sawmill running. Darcy Whitney would stop by two or three times a week to look things over, provide advice, and talk business with Randy and Billy. Darcy would have his men haul much of the rough lumber to his kiln shed for drying, and produce the finely milled oak, pine, and walnut to meet Billy's specifications. Billy would pay for this work with rough cut lumber from his mill.

Four months later Billy and Betty Jane were married. Betty Jane's parents rode the trains from Boston to Sacramento. It took them three ½ days at a cost of $150. Evelyn Richards was Betty Jane's maid of honor and Billy's best man was Robert Gregor. Robert Gregor was the young ranch hand who greeted Billy on his first arrival at the Richards Ranch and would later marry Evelyn Richards.

Billy was anxious to establish a cattle operation on his ranch. His Uncle Will suggested he speak with one of his friends who owned a new breed called Red Dane. Billy would learn the animal was crossbred successfully for both dairy and beef production. It adapted to varying climates and was slightly larger than the average dairy cow in the west. Their fertility rating was exceptionally good, their calving intervals were just under thirteen weeks, and were said to be problem free. They were indeed a powerful breed, and most important, there was a limited number in the Sacramento area. Billy purchased three hundred head.

Time had dealt a heavy blow to Glen Forrester. He was sixty-two years old with no place he could call home. He was only twenty years old when he gave his life to the moving settlers across the plains. Glen had the scars and pains to show for it. With Ben Thompson's help he had finally made it back to Independence, Missouri.

He was sitting in the lobby of a rundown hotel, "The One Day Stay," when they asked him to make one more trip to California. The trip had been made without any major difficulties, but the daily grind had taken it out of Glen. He was finished and there was no doubt about it. He would never make the trip back.

The night after their arrival in Sacramento, Glen was seated in "The Green Onion," a bar-like restaurant on the outer edge of the city. Suddenly, a young middle-aged man with a beard stood before him. Glen was frightened, what had he done wrong? They stared at each other for a moment. Glen said, "What can I do for you?" The young man looked deeply into Glen's eyes and simply said "Glen." When he said Glen's name, Glen knew instantly who he was. Glen had a lump in his throat, but answered, "Billy." Glen stood to shake Billy's hand, but Billy grabbed Glen and embraced him. There was a peaceful sensation that went through Glen he could not understand. It was like he belonged to something beautiful beyond words and both felt it.

Not much was said about the years between their last meeting; that would take place later. But Billy could tell by Glen's appearance things were difficult for Glen. Billy went right to the point. "Where are you staying?" Glen answered, "The livery stable attendant down the way gave me the hayloft for the evening."

This time the lump was in Billy's throat. He looked straight at Glen and spoke in a soft clear voice, "No you're not, you're going home with me." Glen responded, "You can't do that, you're married. What would she say?" Billy answered, "She would disown me if I don't bring you home with me, let's go."

There was no use arguing. Billy always was right in his decisions, and Glen for some reason found himself wanting to go with Billy. They were in a two-seat buckboard tailing a sharp little mare quarter horse going to where Glen had no idea. He wondered what lay ahead of him. At that moment Glen, for some reason he did not understand, felt no worry about tomorrow. Glen seemed to have left his worries about tomorrow at the restaurant where he met Billy.

Presently they came to an archway suspended overhead. It had a print on it, but Glen's eyesight had gotten poor, and he could not read it at dusk. At Billy's prompting Glen talked about the Dreher's, the Heilman's, and of course, Ben Thompson. He also gave all he knew about Jimmy, Isaiah, Melvin, and Jeremy.

At that, Glen paused for a moment, then without any transition of thought he said, "I thought we were done for that day. I had heard of that band before. They did not leave anyone, or anything alive. You young whippersnappers shot them to ribbons." Glen did not need a transition; Billy knew exactly what he was talking about.

After a good half hour at a trotting pace, they pulled up to a large, tall ranch house. Billy stepped down, helping Glen, and handing the reins of the horse to a young Ranch hand. Billy led Glen to the front door and brought Glen in with him.

Billy said in a strong voice, "Betty Jane, I brought someone home with me."

Without any delay a beautiful young lady appeared. She looked directly at Glen, and a moment of recognition hit both she and Glen. Betty Jane came rushing up to Glen and stood before him, "I don't remember ever having seen you before, but I know who you are, you're Glen Forester." Then she threw her arms about him almost squeezing the life out of him.

Once again Glen knew something important and beautiful was happening to him. Glen said, "I saw you in Independence. And I told Billy there was the most beautiful girl I had ever seen on that California wagon train, didn't I Billy." Billy smiled, and looking at Betty Jane, he said, "You were right Glen." Betty Jane looked at Billy, "You never told me that." Billy looked comically at her and responded, "Man does not tell everything he knows."

Both men were hungry, Mary Jane announced the evening meal would be served in fifteen minutes. Billy took Glen to the bunkhouse. It was filled with twelve young men who were very inquisitive in sizing up Glen. Billy introduced Glen to each.

Before Billy and Glen could leave, one fired a last question at Glen, "Were you with the boss on the wagon train?" Glen looked around, realizing how eager they were, and he responded with a smile, "That will make a good bedtime story." That evening, rather than the usual card game, twelve young men would listen intently to some of the story. They would be some of the many men who wished they could relive stories of the Old West. They would have many questions for Glen, and what they heard would be passed on to others. After Billy assigned Glen a bunk, he had to stop any further conversation. He and Glen returned to the ranch house.

Billy ushered Glen into the dining room where there was a large dining table. Glen took note of Betty Jane and four youth who were standing in their respective places at the table which had an open space. Glen knew it must be his. Then Glen's eyes came to rest on a little fellow and without thinking, Glen uttered, "Why he's a spitting image of Billy." This brought a round of laughter from the other three children. Billy and Betty Jane only smiled at the frequently made statement. The little fellow ducked when the other children laughed. Glen gave the little fellow a wink with his good eye, the sight of which made all the children laugh, including the little fellow

Then Billy with dignity introduced Mr. Glen Forester to the children. In unison they responded, "Hello Mr. Forester". Billy then turned to Glen. Glen, on your right is Jacob William McGovern. Across from you, are out twin girls, Maty Jane is on your right and Mill Jean is on your left.

Glen then turned quickly to the little fellow next to him, "And what is your name". In a very innocent manner the little fellow answered, "Glen Forester McGovern." Glen was so moved he stepped from the room into an adjacent hallway to gain his composure.

When he left the room little Glen ask Billy, "Daddy why did he leave the room." Billy answered, "Because you are named after him." Little Glen Commented, "I am glad I am named after him, I like him. " Glen Forester was coming back into the room and he heard what Little Glen had said. From there on they were called Glen senior and Glen junior. And there was a close relationship between the two Glens.

Glen would come to know something else he had missed all his life; he would experience being loved by a family. He would come to know he was a part of the family.

Later, all assembled in the large living room which was the base and focal point of the home. Glen took a moment to survey the room; The room was rectangular in shape and stunning to Glen in size. Glen judged the floor space to be thirty by thirty feet, with a ceiling of at least thirty feet, extending all the way to what Glen was sure was the base of the third floor.

The second story was marked by a walkway surrounding the entire second floor. There was an open railing on the outer edge of the walkway overlooking the area where Glen was standing. The railings and beams were built with beautiful blends of different oak.

It was not the design of the building which caught Glen's eye, he had seen it once before, it was the combination of the different blended oaks that together made its design so attractive and unusual. Glen was not an educated person in such matters, but he knew he was visualizing a rare type of beauty. Glen would learn later it was Betty Jane's unique talent and she was the one who had put the pieces together.

Billy watched Glen admire the construction of the room and fine craftsmanship. he said "Glen, Betty Jane designed the work you see before you. She has a remarkable talent and taste for things that are beautiful. The mixture of the different oaks that appear on the railing are an indication of her insight in putting together the combinations of colors. It is not unusual for us to have visitors for the sole purpose of viewing what Betty Jane has done."

Betty Jane's talent was well known, and the men and women of the Sacramento area frequently sought to get acquainted with Billy and Betty Jane, hoping for an invite to see their property both in and out.

As Glen's vision came from the near vaulted type ceiling down to the main floor, he noticed a piano below the staircase. Billy told the story of how Hilda Swearengen had written to Billy and Betty two years earlier, about a month before the piano arrived in Sacramento. Their son, Raymond, and his wife Marigold had taken over the McGovern's former property.

In fact, Hilda had expressed her pride in the young couple. "Raymond had another very profitable year. He and Marigold have been so pleased with their farm." Raymond had discussed this same thing with Marigold. He suggested "Maybe we can let Billy and his wife know how much the farm, the house, and all the property mean to us." Marigold thought about it, and said "Raymond, I have an idea. The piano sitting in our living room is gathering dust. Can you imagine what that would mean to Billy? Why don't we ship it to them before Christmastime?" Raymond answered, "That is a wonderful idea Marigold, we will do just that."

Billy, Betty Jane, and the family were pleased to receive the piano. They were amazed when Mary Jane played a simple melody for them. When asked where she learned to play. She simply said, "On the back of the kitchen range." Mary Jane had that rare gift. She could hear the music in her mind and even sense the intervals and the difference in pitch between two musical sounds.

She would later take lessons and the family would discover she had inherited her grandmother's gift. Since there was an assortment of good singing voices in the rest of the family, it was always a pleasure to enjoy family music sessions.

Glen had always loved piano playing, and when he said so, Betty Jane nodded to Mary Jane. Mary Jane asked Glen, "Mr. Forester. Do you have a song you favor?" Glen said, "There is a song something about "Take me home again Kathleen." Mary Jane had no problem in playing the tune requested. Truthfully, there had been a young lady in Glen's past named Kathleen. The memories and song were special to Glen. He and the family clapped when Mary Jane completed her song.

Glen turned toward the glowing fireplace and expansive mantel area where a number of items were very neatly and attractively displayed. He rose from his chair and walked across the room for a closer look.

They were items that Glen recognized immediately. There was a buffalo robe which held the center position above the mantel. Directly under the robe was a polished 1860 Henry rifle. There was a beautiful folded red shirt with the words "Red Shirt" embroidered across the left pocket. There was a .45 Colt in holster, still well-preserved. There was a beautiful turquoise stone attached to a worn deer skin lope. And last, but displayed in such manner that was not least, were two buckskin leather straps displayed on a small cleverly cut piece of oak. Under the straps were two beautifully scripted words, "Lone Eagle."

Billy knew Glen had seen all the other objects and knew exactly where they came from, and what they meant. When Glen's gaze rested on the two little buckskin straps with the words "Lone Eagle" printed underneath.

Betty Jane spoke. "I was so shaken and frightened when Lone Eagle gave his life for me. The ugly little man, I knew what he had planned for me, when Lone Eagle came from nowhere. I knew Lone Eagle took a bullet, but it never stopped him. He took the little man's knife and did to the little man what I had seen that ugly little man do to several women and children on the wagon train."

Glen added, "Three Bears told the entire story later. Mourning Dove, a young Choctaw maiden, had heard him give the account which came from reading sign left on the earth.

Three Bears knew Red Shirt and the young white eyes girl had escaped. Three Bears knew Red Shirt had built Lone Eagle's burial platform. In death, Lone Eagle carried the look of a warrior who won his battle." Billy, Betty Jane, and the children all knew what Lone Eagle had done for them. The two little buckskin straps on the mantel would remind them.

The truth was Billy and Betty Jane's two girls had wanted a part in decorating, and though Billy and Betty Jane were not overly enthusiastic about the girl's choice of the mantel decoration, the girls had presented an attractive collage. Betty was proud of the girls' talented work. She and Billy had allowed it.

Some weeks later, Billy approached Betty Jane with a thought. "Betty Jane, we have that little room on the back of the house with the door leading to the porch..." But before Billy could continue, Betty Jane said, "I know Billy, I bought a rocker the other day." Billy smiled to himself and scratched his head thinking, "Why do women always know what you're thinking even before you bring it up?" Then Billy, hoping to gain an edge in the conversation, acting like nothing had happened, posed a question to Betty Jane, "How soon would it take you to get it ready?" "It's been ready for two weeks," was the reply. This time it was Betty Jane who gave Billy a big smile. Billy walked over and kissed Betty Jane, ending the conversation.

Early the next morning Glen Senior moved into the little room on the back of the house. He had just gotten settled when he heard a small little knock on the door. Glen had a hunch he knew who it was. Glen waited to see if the knock would come again. Sure enough, it did. Glen asked, "Who is it?" A tiny little voice responded, "Its me." Glen answered, "Me can come in." Glen Junior came into Senior's room for the first time. The little fellow did not say anything, he just stood in front of Glen Senior. Glen Senior was seated, and he did something he had wanted to do. Reaching out, he pulled little Glen to him, and embraced him.

Glen senior did not see the ear-to-ear smile on little Glen's face.

THE END

EPILOGUE

Twelve years after Glen Juniors first visit with Glen Senior, six grief-stricken people met on a wind-swept hill over - looking a grave site. There was a beautiful stone with the words neatly carved.

Glen Forester
BORN DEC. 5, 1818
DIED   APR.10, 1892

It was a fitting goodbye to a man who had meant so much to Billy, Betty Jane and their children. Glen had contributed to the children's character. They had loved him like family. Glen Junior, now seventeen years old, would miss him most.

THE END

Made in the USA
Middletown, DE
06 December 2023